A LIFE FOR NANCY

THE DAUGHTER OF

FRANKIE SILVER

A LIFE FOR NANCY — THE DAUGHTER OF FRANKIE SILVER

BY

DANITA STOUDEMIRE

AND

RILEY HENRY

Cover/Back Graphics Design by
MICHAEL M. ROGERS
(www.sharethebeauty.tv)

Frankie Silver and Nancy Parker Portrayed on Cover
By TARA and CHANNING RAY

www.bookstandpublishing.com

Published by
Bookstand Publishing
Morgan Hill, CA 95037
3700_2

ISBN 978-1-61863-333-0

Library of Congress Control Number: 2012913256

Printed in the United States of America

Dedicated to Nancy's great-great-granddaughter,
Wanda Henry.
Thank you for your memories. We could not have done
it without you!
Nancy would be proud.

CHAPTER ONE

JANUARY 1832

It was a bitter cold January night as the wagon rumbled across the frozen ground. Jacob Stuart had hoped for a night like this, for he knew that if he could get across the French Broad River before daylight his chances of making it on home to Ellijay would be good.

Jacob and his wife, Elizabeth, sure hadn't anticipated making a journey to Toe River in Burke County so soon after the Christmas holiday, but circumstances gave them no other choice. Jacob's cousin, Frankie, was in trouble, and he had to do all he could to help her. Of course at this point there wasn't much he could do for Frankie, but he could take her 13-month-old daughter, Nancy, and keep her from the Silver family.

The moon was bright as Jacob made his way along the old road that led to the river while Nancy slept. He knew Elizabeth would get no rest; she was too worried about the Silver men catching up to them. He was worried too, but he knew that once they got across the river no one would know which way they went.

All the Silver family knew about Frankie's family was that they lived to the west. They had often heard her beg Charlie to go west and live near her cousin. That could be anywhere in these mountains. All the trails led to small towns, but they were great distances apart from each other, over rivers and rock cliffs that were sometimes almost impossible to get around. It was very rough country to say the least, and Charlie had never cared enough about traveling it to ever ask exactly where it was that Jacob lived.

1

Everything had been quiet for awhile as Jacob listened to the wagon wheels crunch against the frozen dirt. It sure gave him time to think about what he was doing. Who would have thought that he would be caught up in a murder of all things? Frankie had been married to Charlie Silver for just little more than a year. He hadn't seen her since then, because the only decent road between Ellijay and Toe River was a five-day trip by wagon. He had thought that Charlie was a good man or Frankie wouldn't of married him, but family gossip said otherwise.

Frankie was only 17 years old and Charlie 18, when they married. At first they were like any other married couple. Charlie built them a cabin near Frankie's folks in Stuart Cove and just over the ridge from his mom and dad in Toe River. He spent his days chopping wood and taking care of the little farm they had made for themselves. But, as cold weather neared, he got restless and got to drinking and staying gone for days on end. Even after Nancy was born that same year, in November, Frankie was mostly alone. She stayed home and cared for the house and the baby and tried hard to make Charlie happy when he did come in from his long, so-called hunting trips. She knew he wasn't always hunting when he said he was. She had heard about him running around with them trampy women that lifted their skirts for a man whether he was married or not. Charlie was a good looking feller, but for the life of Jacob, he couldn't understand why he would want other women when Frankie was quite a beauty herself. She was a short little thing, with long flowing dark hair, chickipen eyes and mahogany skin. What man wouldn't want her for his wife? But, apparently, Charlie wasn't happy with her, and he let her know this often, according to what everybody said.

Word had it that Frankie, as hot-tempered a young woman as she was, even feared away from him when he would come home in a drunken stupor and take a stick to her, beating her over some selfish act that she had or had not committed. The one time she threatened to get the sheriff on him, he just laughed at her and called her a stupid bitch. "Don't you know it ain't against the law for a man to whip his woman in this state as long as the stick ain't no bigger around than his finger?" He had spat at her, his breath no doubt wreaking of hard liquor.

"No bigger than a finger my foot," Jacob thought, as he heard a low cry in the back of the wagon. He needed to stop for a minute anyway. All this thinking had made his blood run plumb hot on this frigid night.

Jacob pulled the horses to a stop, got out of the wagon and peeked in to make sure everything was alright. Elizabeth lay on her side on a stack of quilts on the floor of the wagon with Nancy cuddled in her arms. Wisps of brown hair from under her bonnet hung in her eyes, and she looked rather pale in the bright moonlight.

"You alright?" Jacob asked quietly.

Elizabeth just nodded her head, so as not to wake the baby.

"The way I figure, it's about another hour to the French Broad River," he said. "We'll probably be passin' a lot of other folk as we git near on into Asheville, so you need to keep Nancy quiet."

She nodded her head again, but her eyes were filled with sorrow. He knew she was worried and tired. "Everything's gonna be alright," he said rather sternly, so she would believe him. "You just try and git some sleep, you hear."

Elizabeth trusted her husband, and she knew things would work out. But, she was tired and hungry. Her weary bones ached from the

3

jolting of the wagon wheels against the ruts in the road. It may have been different if she and Jacob were young, but already they were past fifty with grown children of their own and even grandchildren. They were tough old mountain people, to say the least, but traveling still took its toll on them. Elizabeth almost wished she was walking, that seemed a whole lot easier than riding in this bumpy old wagon. But none of that mattered right now because family needed them, and it didn't matter how far away they were or how hard it was to get there, it was up to them to do what they thought was right to help.

She looked down at the sleeping baby in her arms and thought about how she would grow up. Her father, Charlie, was dead. No one knew if she would ever see her mother, Frankie, again. If not, how would she and Jacob ever be able to tell her that her mother had been the one accused of killing her father. Such a sad, sad story. And, what a beautiful child Nancy was. She had the same dark hair and skin that her mother had, and oh those eyes. They just melted Elizabeth's very heart. She snuggled Nancy closer and vowed to never let no harm come to her and to always keep her in the Stuart family, no matter what it took.

With that thought in mind, Elizabeth closed her eyes and let sleep finally come to her.

Daylight was upon them when the French Broad River came into sight. Jacob was relieved that no one seemed to pay them any attention. Folks probably just thought he was headed back home from spending Christmas with distant relatives. As a matter of fact, that's exactly what he would tell them, if anybody bothered to ask. He would travel upriver a short distance from the ferry and ford across so that if anyone came to ask about them later, no one at the ferry would know what they were talking about. For a split second, Jacob wondered why he was so worried. After all, Nancy was his family too. What right did it give the Silvers to think that they should raise Frankie's daughter? Frankie didn't want it that way, she had made that very clear. But, right now, all Jacob knew was that Frankie was in jail, along with her mother, Barbara, and her brother, Blackston, while her dad, Isaiah, was trying to figure out a way to get them out. Damndest thing he had ever heard of.

He and Elizabeth had been enjoying what was left of the Christmas holiday when suddenly everything was disrupted. Jackson Stuart, Frankie's older brother, came pounding on the door. It was some time before they could get him calmed down enough to figure out what he was trying to say. Then, he told them that Charlie had been killed and Frankie and his mom and brother were in jail accused of it. Charlie's dad and stepmother had taken Nancy, and Frankie didn't want them to have her. She had spoken with Jackson about a plan she had. He was to come to Ellijay, fetch Jacob and Elizabeth, and bring them to Toe River. Then he was to figure out how to get Nancy away from the Silvers and take her back home with them until all of this was over with. Frankie was convinced that she would be found innocent of Charlie's death and when that happened, she would just move to Ellijay herself and put all this ugly mess behind her.

So that's exactly what Jacob and Elizabeth had done. They left out the very next morning and traveled to Toe River. Since Jackson knew the layout of the Silver home, having been there many times, he planned to go in during the night, pick up the sleeping baby and carry her away on horseback to where Jacob and Elizabeth would be waiting in the wagon at the forks of the road. Everything had went according to plan, except they had not expected old man Silver to wake up.

5

He chased Jackson with a shotgun, yelling at him and firing into the night air, "I'll find you, you son of a bitch and when I do, I'll blow your brains out. You bring that baby back. You hear me!" He shouted till he couldn't shout no more. Jacob Silver may have been a preacher man, but Jackson was sure that, had he not been holding Nancy, the old man would have shot him.

By the time he got to the wagon, Nancy was crying something furious. Elizabeth wrapped her in a quilt and quickly gathered her into the back of the wagon. Jacob slapped the horses hard with the reins, guiding them down the right fork of the road towards Morganton, while Jackson rode off to the left towards Stuart Cove. He felt sure that once Jacob Silver got his clothes on and his horse saddled, he would head that way thinking that Nancy had been taken to the Stuart's house.

Jacob sure hoped Jackson had been right in his thinking. They had traveled toward Morganton, took another fork in the road towards Burnsville and made their way by moonlight across the rugged terrain into Asheville, and now, finally, they were crossing the French Broad River.

It was almost too easy, Jacob thought. He could only imagine the uproar going on in Toe River. Old man Silver probably recognized Jackson, if he got a good look at him. Without a doubt he would know it was a Stuart who had kidnapped Nancy and would go looking for her. They would go to the Morganton jail house and question Frankie and her mom and brother. Then they would try to get Isaiah to tell them where he was hiding her. They would eventually find Jackson, but he would swear on his own life that he had nothing to do with it. It was all about family, and Jacob knew that no one, not the sheriff, not the judge, not Jesus Christ himself, would get a word out of any of them, and once he got across the river, they would be home free, and he could go on about his business in Ellijay. Nobody would ever look for Nancy there. Even if they came as far as Franklin, it wouldn't matter because not many folks knew anything about Ellijay, and they sure didn't travel there because the road was bad even in good weather.

The splash of the water and the sudden movement of the wagon woke Elizabeth and the baby. Once across the river, Jacob turned the team to the left and traveled a short distance to a small field. He pulled the wagon out of sight into a grove of pines in the corner. This is where they would rest for a spell and get something to eat before traveling on into Waynesville. As he unhooked the horses from the wagon, Elizabeth carried Nancy outside, and breathed a sigh of relief.

CHAPTER TWO
MAY 1833

Jacob had been plowing the field all day. Every now and then he would stop and look towards the house to catch a glimpse of Nancy running through the yard. It was hard to believe that already she had been with them for more than a year. There were many nights that she had cried for her mother as Elizabeth cuddled her against her breast and sang sweet lullabies in her ear till she fell asleep. There was no way of explaining to a child so young the tragedy that had befallen her parents. Someday she would have to know the truth, but right now, the important thing was to let her know she was loved and raise her the best way they knew how.

The sound of horses hooves interrupted Jacob's thoughts. He dropped his plow and ran toward the house, scooping Nancy up in his arms as Elizabeth stood in the doorway.

"Git her inside," he said, as he handed Nancy to Elizabeth. "Don't come out till I tell you to."

With that, he shut the door and watched from the stoop as the man came closer. No unexpected visitors had darkened his door since they had brought Nancy here. Why would they? Ellijay was a very remote part of Macon County. The road leading to their house had many twists and turns, with steep drop offs on each side in some places. It wasn't easy to get to, and not many people tried unless it was family, and that wasn't very often.

Jacob kept a steady gaze on the young man as he dismounted his horse, took off his hat and approached the porch asking, "Are you Jacob Stuart?"

"Who wants to know?" Jacob questioned, never taking his eyes off the young man. His clothes were wrinkled and covered in dust, and he seemed in a hurry as he dismounted his horse and came toward Jacob.

"The name's Erwin," he said, extending his hand in a friendly gesture. "Lester Erwin, sir. Isaiah Stuart sent me."

Jacob didn't move. How did he know this was true? Isaiah was Jacob's uncle, and Frankie's father. Last he had heard about Isaiah, he was still trying to get Frankie out of jail in Morganton. He had succeeded in getting the release of her mother and brother when they could find no solid proof that they had helped Frankie kill Charlie.

"Git to the point, boy," Jacob said, without returning the handshake.

"Anyway," Lester stammered. "Like I said, sir, Isaiah Stuart sent me to git you. The judge has set the date for Frankie to be hanged June 28. Isaiah has plans to break her out of jail, but he needs you to come and git her. He figures she'd be safe here."

Jacob was trying hard to take it all in. Apparently, there was more to this story than he knew. Living so far away didn't give a lot of access to the news, and since he had taken Nancy, his relatives living in the Toe River area didn't want to send letters in fear of the Silvers finding out where she was.

"Come on in," Jacob finally said, opening the door for the stranger.

Elizabeth stood in the kitchen clutching Nancy to her.

"It's okay," Jacob told her. "I need you to pack me and this young feller some food. I have to go to Morganton for a few days." He didn't really want to tell her why he was going, but he could see the question in her eyes.

"Isaiah needs me. They're gonna hang Frankie."

Elizabeth gasped. Jacob pulled her to him, assuring her that he would be back and everything would be okay.

Jacob saddled his horse, gathered up the few things he would need for the journey and the food Elizabeth had packed for him. As they rode away, Jacob told Lester that he thought it would be wise to go get his son-in-law, Abe Moore, who lived a short distance down the road. Abe was married to Jacob and Elizabeth's daughter, Lydia. Shortly after they had brought Nancy to Ellijay, Abe had went to Morganton to sign a petition for Frankie's release from jail.

Just as Jacob figured, Abe was more than willing to go with them to get Frankie. He firmly believed that she was innocent, and besides that, he didn't want poor little Nancy growing up without her momma.

As the three men mounted their horses, Abe suggested that they take the trail over to Pine Creek, across Yellow Mountain into Cashiers and from there to Hendersonville on into Rutherford County, which was just this side of Morganton. This route, he explained, was a lot quicker and the terrain was rugged, so they wouldn't likely meet up with anyone. Jacob and Lester agreed that would be the best way to travel and they would take that same way back home. As they rode, Lester explained that he didn't know exactly how Isaiah had gotten Frankie out of jail, but he knew that she would be hiding out at his two old maid sisters' house. Then, when things settled down, Jacob was to take her to Ellijay to be with Nancy.

They rode hard through the night into the next evening, stopping very little until they arrived in Morganton. They went straight to

Lester's sisters' house so no one would see them. Jacob was taking a huge risk. Even though he had not actually been the one who took Nancy from the Silver's home, he was still a part of her kidnapping. And now, even though he wasn't the one to actually break Frankie out of jail, he would still be a part of her escape.

Frankie was waiting for them at the Erwin sisters. She had cut her long, dark hair, and she looked frail. Jacob could only guess the toil the last year had taken on his young cousin. Few women had ever been where Frankie had, locked up in a prison where bread and beans was the only means of filling your stomach, not to mention the dirty stares and vulgar mouths of drunken men who passed her bars. She had no privacy whatsoever, and all she could do was hope that someone with the importance to free her would believe that she was innocent.

Her first questions to Jacob were about Nancy. She had to know every detail of what had been going on with her young child. She missed her so terribly that sometimes, while lying on the hard mattress they called a bed in jail, she felt like her heart would surely break. At least she knew Nancy was safe and, hopefully, she would soon be able to hold her in her arms.

Jacob and Abe stayed for a few days, while Lester made his way around town like he always did, keeping a sharp ear out for any word about Frankie. Oh they were looking for her alright, but, so far, they had found nothing.

Finally, Jacob decided it was time to go. It was now or never. They could stay hid out here for months, but it wouldn't change the fact that they eventually needed to get Frankie to Ellijay. He and the Erwin sisters dressed Frankie as a boy so as not to draw attention to her and, when it got good and dark, they hooked the horses up to an old wagon

12

that the sisters had in the shed. They filled the back of the wagon with hay for Frankie to hide under and made their way back toward Rutherford County.

They traveled through the night unnoticed, and as morning dawned, Frankie decided it was time for her to get out and walk for a ways. They hadn't seen anyone in hours and she had been hid under the hay all night. The cool morning air felt good on Frankie's skin as she walked along side the wagon making small talk with Jacob and Abe. She knew she was far from being safe yet, but this was as close to freedom as she had felt in a long time. She breathed in a long, slow breath of the fresh air and closed her eyes, savoring this moment in her mind forever.

The morning was still. An old crow flew over them and cawed. The three of them watched the bird land in a tree nearby. They believed in the superstitions of the mountains they had heard tell of all their lives, and they all thought the black crow was a bad omen. They were all fearing the same thing when, in the stillness of the morning, they heard the sound of horses hooves coming quick.

"No, it can't be," Frankie thought, as she scrambled for the back of the wagon. But, it was too late. Several riders approached them and surrounded the wagon. Jacob knew they were caught. There was no way around it, unless these men just didn't recognize Frankie with her short hair and boy clothes.

"Where you headed?" one of the men asked Jacob, as he reined his horse in next to the wagon, just close enough that Jacob could see the badge under his coat. Jacob kept the wagon moving at a steady pace, trying to keep his eyes on the trail in front of them.

"Headed to Cowpens, South Caliner," he said calmly. "Takin' this here boy down that way to work for his uncle for the summer."

"That true, boy?" he asked Frankie, who was setting on the back of the wagon, legs dangling and boots kicking up dust under her heels.

She never looked up as fear gripped her very soul. She had to remain calm or the freedom she had felt only moments before would be gone forever. She gripped the wagon and shut her eyes tight, never lifting her head as she answered in as deep a voice as she could muster up, "yes sir."

A smirk came across his face. "Look at me boy when I'm talkin' to you." He spit on the ground beside her.

Slowly, Frankie lifted her eyes to meet the gaze of the sheriff. She didn't even have to think about her next move. She jumped from the wagon and took off running down the trail. But, it was no good. Several of the others were off their horses and caught up to her before she could get very far. One of them picked her up. She was kicking and screaming, fighting for her very life, "I ain't goin' back I tell you! I ain't goin' back!"

Jacob and Abe were trying to get to her, but the others detained them both, throwing them on the ground and holding guns on them. It was no use. They all knew it. No matter how much fighting and screaming they did, it wasn't gonna do any good. Tears streaked the dirt on Frankie's face. She just didn't know how much more fight she had left in her, but she would never give up. Somehow, she would find a way back to her daughter.

The sheriff ordered the three of them into the back of the wagon and they all headed back to Morganton. They rode silently as the sheriff tried to get answers from Frankie about her escape. But she wouldn't give them anything. She knew that without her testimony to the fact, neither her father, nor Jacob, nor Abe could be tried as accessories to her escape.

Once in Morganton, the two men were locked in a cell, and Frankie was taken away separately. Deep inside, Jacob had this gut feeling that he would never see his cousin again. She must have felt it too, for as she was taken away, she called out to Jacob, "There's somethin' in my bag in the wagon. Give it to Nancy some day, when she's old enough."

He could see the tears in her eyes. "What is it? What am I lookin' for?"

She jerked away from her captives and looked at Jacob. Right now he was the only connection she had to Nancy. "It's my hair," she could barely whisper as her voice cracked and she broke down, crying out everything that had been pent up in her for months. She had tried so hard to be strong. She had spit on them when they tried to get her to tell them her mom and brother had helped her kill Charlie. She had refused to eat for days on end when they tried to put words in her mouth, telling her how they thought she had killed her husband. They didn't know nothing. No one knew anything about that night in her cabin. Everyone was guessing and making up tales -- mean, evil tales that weren't true. She would have her day -- or perhaps she would never have her day -- either way, no one would ever really know the whole truth. She would take it to her grave with her. She knew that there was no way out. She would be punished for the crime and no one, not even her father, could save her now.

The next morning, Jacob and Abe were released. In the wagon, hidden under the hay, was a small sack that had a dress and a comb in it and there, wrapped in a piece of paper with writing on it, was a ponytail of Frankie's hair held together with a piece of string. Jacob carefully folded the paper and put it in his pocket. He would make sure Nancy got it when the time was right.

The two men headed back to Ellijay empty handed, their hearts heavy, but their heads held high. Someone, and they would never know who, had tipped the sheriff off or he would have never known where to look for them. They had tried to set Frankie free, just like so many other people had by signing petitions for her release and writing letters to the governor. But, it seemed her fate was in the hands of the Silver family, just like it had been from the beginning.

CHAPTER THREE

APRIL 1836

It had been three years since Jacob had tried to bring Frankie to Ellijay. He thought of her often after that day, but try as he may, he could think of no way to save her from the gallows. And, on July 12, 1833, she was hanged; not even two months after she had breathed a small breath of freedom on the trail that day. He and Abe had went back to Morganton for the hanging. It was a sad, sad day, one that neither man would ever forget.

Nancy was now five years old and had adjusted well to living in Ellijay. She had Jacob and Elizabeth's grandchildren to play with, and she seemed content.

Jacob and Elizabeth talked about her mother often. They wanted her to know how much Frankie had wanted her and they instilled all the memories they could into her little mind. Someday, she would have to know that her mother had been hanged for killing her father, but right now none of that mattered.

The Silvers had never given up on looking for Nancy. They just didn't know where to go in search of her. Even if they had known, their energy was eventually spent and they were still convinced that, somewhere, some of Frankie's family had their granddaughter. They knew that none of the Stuarts living in Toe River had her for they had been searched many times. But, beyond that, they had no clue where else to look. They had heard many times that she had been taken west. But that could mean anywhere. Actually, they didn't even know for sure that Frankie's own parents knew where Nancy was.

But, they knew -- Isaiah and Barbara Stuart knew exactly where she was. They just wasn't about to tell anyone. But, as the years passed, Barbara just couldn't find peace. She missed her girl terribly and worried every day that the Silvers would find her granddaughter. The thought of losing her too was more than Barbara could bear. Several times she had pleaded with Isaiah to help her get custody of Nancy, but he insisted that it would come to no good, and it was best to leave it alone. Now he was on his deathbed, and soon she would be losing him too. It was just too much for her. Why couldn't she get her granddaughter back? So far as she knew, the Silver family had given up on looking for her. They were getting on up in years, but she knew, without a doubt, that she still had enough fight left in her to do what she had to do to give Nancy a home like her momma had wanted. With that, it was decided. She would just go file for custody herself, and she wouldn't tell a soul until it was done.

It was actually easier than Barbara had planned and for once, it seemed the courts were on her side. It had not been an easy way for the Stuarts in Toe River. They heard the whispers of neighbors and the snide remarks that never seemed to go away. They were murderers themselves in the eyes of some folks, even though they hadn't swung the ax that killed Charlie. Of course, they had tried to help their daughter in every way they could, who wouldn't have? But try telling these mountain people that. They'd sit on their porches, spitting tobacco for hours on end, trying to figure out the truth of the situation, laying blame where it shouldn't of been laid and even making up their own version of what happened.

Barbara was sick of it all. She just wanted it to go away and she wanted a little bit of happiness in this godforsaken life she had been living. The people who had took pity on Frankie knew how Barbara must feel, and some of these people were the very ones who helped her draw up the petition for Nancy. Not everyone held the Silvers in as high regard as they liked to think they were. There were a lot of folks who wanted Frankie freed and cried self-defense for her, wrote the governor letters and showed up during her trial to plead her innocence. It didn't work for Frankie, but now they could make it work for Nancy.

Barbara told them everything. She told them that she knew where Nancy was and she wanted her back, free and clear -- legally. And she let them know at the courthouse that she would go to great lengths to make this happen. They had taken her daughter, her husband was dying and she had nothing much else to live for, unless she could raise her granddaughter.

The judge listened to her intently and, without argument, granted the petition. No one in the Silver family had ever come forward to lay claim to Nancy anyway, so why shouldn't Barbara Stuart have her? She was beside herself as she made her way home to tell Isaiah.

She had the papers in her hand that said Nancy was to be given "at least one year of schooling and upon turning the age of 18 is to receive one cow and calf, two suits of clothes, one good bed and furniture." When Barbara entered the house, she knew immediately that something was wrong. Isaiah sat slumped over in his chair and she could smell death all around her. She dropped the papers to the floor as she knelt beside him and took his feeble hand in hers.

"Isaiah," she whispered. "Isaiah, I did it. I can bring Nancy here to live with us now. You'll see, it'll be alright."

Isaiah tried to lift his head to look at her, but it was no use. His life was over. He would take to his grave all that he knew about his daughter and he hoped Barbara would do the same. But right now, he knew she was happier than she had been in a long time and, for an instant, thought that perhaps he had been wrong in not getting Nancy back a long time ago.

"Take care of the girl," he whispered, as he took his last breath.

Barbara sat on the floor beside him for a few minutes. Oh, she cried alright. She couldn't help it. This was the man who had stood beside her through all these tough times, the man she loved and had her children with. This was the man who had tried every way in the world to save his daughter. Now she was on her own. But she was strong, and she had a mean streak in her a mile long when need be, so she knew she would be alright. She was a mountain woman through and through. She had just proven that to herself and all who knew her.

She stood up and brushed herself off, picked up the papers and headed down the road to get her boy, Jackson, to come and help her make preparations for Isaiah's burial.

The next day, she sent word to Jacob and Elizabeth that Isaiah had died and that she was taking legal custody of Nancy. Jacob and Elizabeth had grown so accustomed to having Nancy that they didn't really want to give her up. But they both knew that this was what Frankie would want if she were still alive. Besides, perhaps she would have a better life in Toe River. There were more people there; she could go to school and make lots of friends. They could visit her often and when she got older she could visit them. There was just no way they could keep her from her grandmother, it just wouldn't be right. But, oh how Elizabeth grieved. It was like giving up one of her own children. Her heart was broken as they packed up Nancy's few belongings and headed out on the long trip to Toe River. At least winter was past them, and they would have fairly warm weather to travel in. They would stay a few days with Barbara and the rest of Jacob's kinfolk, then journey back home to Ellijay. Already, Elizabeth felt lost. She knew that only time would heal that which was being taken from her.

CHAPTER FOUR

1836–1847

Nancy settled in quite well with her grandmother and Barbara loved having her there. It helped her pass the days and keep her mind off things in the past. She talked to Nancy often about her mother. She wanted her so badly to remember Frankie, but in her heart knew that was impossible as young as she had been when she was taken from her. Still, she would do her best, and when the time was right, she would tell her everything and give her the gift that Frankie had left behind for her.

It wasn't long before word got out in the valley that Nancy was living with Barbara. Nancy and Jacob Silver were furious. Who would have thought that after five years their granddaughter would be living back in Toe River? They immediately went to the courthouse with many questions. But none to their advantage. Truth was, they had not asked for Nancy legally before, so they couldn't lay claim to her now. They had just assumed that some of the Stuarts had her, because they knew it was Jackson who took her that night right out of their own house. But they could never prove that, and none of the Stuarts had talked about her whereabouts. Now there was nothing they could do. The custody hearing was over, and Nancy legally belonged to Barbara Stuart. They could put up a fight, but in the end, who would it benefit? It would only hurt Nancy more, and the poor girl had been put through enough already.

Somehow, they would figure out a way to put their anger for the Stuarts aside just long enough to get to know their granddaughter; then they would tell her their side of the story and what really happened to her parents. They would let her know how much their Charlie had loved her and what a mean, evil woman her mother was. Then, perhaps, Nancy wouldn't grow up to be like her. Meanwhile, they would let it rest, but only for a short time till their paths actually crossed, which was bound to happen soon in a place like Toe River.

Word traveled fast, and soon everybody for miles around knew that Nancy was back, and everybody had their own ideas about where she had been. They had heard the stories from the Silver family about how Nancy had been kidnapped. Most of them had even opened their homes to old Jacob Silver to prove to him they weren't hiding Nancy themselves. At first he blamed everyone on the other side of the creek, whether they were Stuarts or not, for taking Nancy. Eventually though, he had given up and all that was left was whispers amongst the womenfolk about "poor little Nancy."

Barbara and Isaiah had tried hard not to pay any attention to these whispers when Isaiah was alive, so Barbara decided it was best for her to keep it that way now that he was dead. "Let them say what they want to," she thought. She really didn't care anymore. And that's what she told Nancy before she sent her off to school the next fall. "Now don't you go listenin' to what them other kids have to say about your ma, you hear," she told Nancy. "You jest hold your head up and be strong."

"I'll try," Nancy answered, with her eyes on the floor.

She sure was a timid little thing. Try as she may, Barbara couldn't really get her to open up. She smiled sometimes and even laughed sometimes, but mostly it seemed to her that Nancy was in deep thought about something. She hadn't yet told her much about her folks. She was still too young to hear all that. Instead, she just told her the same thing Jacob and Elizabeth had always told her -- that they died in a terrible

24

accident. She knew that eventually Nancy would get old enough to start asking what kind of accident. But for now, she would just leave it alone.

She patted Nancy on the head as she sent her out the door. It wasn't far down the road to the little village school, and she new Nancy would be fine.

And she was fine -- for awhile anyway.

Nancy was content living with her grandmother. She went to school, but she never really made any friends. She was just too quiet. She hung back from the rest of the kids when they would play games and wasn't interested much in making friends.

Sometimes, she would see the older kids pointing at her and whispering and she wondered what they were talking about, but she didn't dare ask. She just went on in her own little world, studying her reading and practicing her handwriting.

Then one day, when she came home from school, there was a strange woman waiting on her. She could tell her grandmother wasn't one bit happy about this woman being there.

"This here's your other granny," she said to Nancy as she came through the door. "She lives on the other side of the creek there, up in the holler."

Nancy didn't say anything, she just looked at the floor.

"Well, say hello to her," Barbara said, nudging Nancy toward the strange woman.

"Hello," she said, so low that she could barely be heard.

The woman lowered herself to her knees so she would be the same height as Nancy. She lifted Nancy's chin up with her finger so their eyes met. Then she smiled. Nancy smiled back, and the woman hugged her long and hard.

With that, the woman stood up and walked out the door. There were no explanations or words exchanged between them or Barbara. They just left it alone for the time. After that Nancy saw her Granny Silver and other kinfolk every now and again. Barbara didn't deny the Silvers seeing her, but she made sure she kept a close eye on them. Sometimes they would see them at the trading post or at the church they occasionally went to and Nancy even found out that she was in school with some of them. They were the ones who talked about her and made fun of her to the other kids.

And, it only got worse as she got older.

Nancy grew to love Grandma Stuart, and she looked forward to the visits from Jacob and Elizabeth. Sometimes they would even bring some of their grandkids with them to play with Nancy. She was very smart in school and, when the 12 months was up that was mentioned in the custody papers, Barbara insisted that Nancy keep going. Her Frankie had been smart, and she wanted Nancy to be smart too.

Gradually, Nancy even made a couple of friends, but for the most part, she was left alone. She didn't really understand why no one wanted to be around her, that's just the way it had always been. The two girls she did play with had just moved to Toe River, and they didn't seem to mind talking to her, but they didn't know who she really was. Everyone else seemed to think she was strange. But she really wasn't strange, she just didn't know where she belonged.

One day when she was just minding her own business at recess, a couple of the older boys started teasing her. These same boys had always been mean to her, pulling her hair and laughing at her all through school, but she was in the fourth grade now and she was tired of it. One of the boys pushed her and, before Nancy even thought about it, she pushed him back. In fact, she pushed him so hard that he staggered backwards, his feet flying out from under him, and he set down right in the middle of the dirt.

Laughter from the other kids stopped as the boy got up, brushed his britches off, and walked up to Nancy. She looked him square in the eyes, determined to stand her ground like Grandma Stuart had always told her to do.

"At least my ma didn't kill my pa," he spat at her.

Nancy didn't know what to say. She stood there glaring at the boy.

"That's right," he snarled. "I said your ma killed your pa."

One of the other boys shouted, "Yea, your ma was a murderer!"

Then, the other kids started joining in, chanting "murderer, murderer, ..." till Nancy couldn't take it anymore. She covered her ears with her hands and took off running down the path toward home. "No, it can't be," she thought. "My folks were killed in an accident." And for the first time, Nancy wondered what kind of accident had taken their lives.

She ran through the front door of Barbara's house, tears streaming down her cheeks. Barbara came out of the kitchen wiping her hands on her apron. Nancy ran to her, throwing her arms around her waist and sobbing her heart out.

Barbara tried to comfort her, drying her tears on her apron and telling her not to worry about it. But Nancy was worried about it. Those kids were mean to her, and she wanted to know why.

"I gotta know," she cried. "The kids at school said ma killed my pa. Is that true? I have to know! Is that why nobody wants to play with me? Is that why nobody likes me and everybody pokes fun of me?"

Barbara knew the time had come. "Dear Lord," she prayed, "let me say the right thing." She had dreaded this day for so long. She had tried to figure out in her mind how she would tell Nancy -- exactly what she would say to her. Now the time had come and she just couldn't tell her everything. How could she? Nancy was still too young for such details of the tragedy. She would only tell her enough to satisfy her.

"It was a terrible accident just like you always been told," she began.

Nancy wiped her eyes and set down beside her grandma. Barbara took her hand and patted it as she continued.

"Now, now. Dry them there tears up," she soothed. "Sometimes, when folks grow up and git married, they don't always git along. And as much as your mommy and daddy loved you, they didn't love each other much, at least not after awhile." Barbara was trying hard to hold back her own tears. She had to be strong like she had always told Nancy to be.

"Anyway, one night they got into a bad fuss. Everybody said that your ma must a thought your pa was gonna hit her, so she picked up the closest thing to her and hit him over the head with it. She didn't mean to kill him, I just know she didn't. But that's what they said happened and because of it, she got in bad trouble and later died."

Nancy couldn't believe what she was hearing. No wonder everybody whispered behind her back. No wonder nobody wanted to be friends with her. No wonder her grandma shielded her from just about everything and everybody.

"When they put your ma in jail is when you went to live with Jacob and Elizabeth," Barbara continued. "Your ma wanted you to stay in the Stuart family. She didn't want the Silver family to have you. She was so afraid they would turn you against her and she couldn't have that, no siree," she went on. "Me and your granddaddy tried every way in the world to save her, but we failed. We promised her that you would always be cared for by somebody in our family."

Now it was silent tears that washed down Nancy's face. She had always been told how much her mother loved her and only occasionally that her father had loved her, too. Now she knew why he wasn't spoken of much.

Barbara sat quietly, letting Nancy take it all in and, at the same time, hoping that she would be satisfied with this story for now and not ask any questions. But, her young mind was reeling and she did have questions -- lots of questions.

"But," she began, as she looked up at Barbara.

"That's all for now Nancy," Barbara said. "You're so young. You have your whole life ahead of you. Now don't you go frettin' about somethin' that happened all them years ago. As time goes, people will forget, and until then, it's like I always told you -- hold your head up and be strong. And you have. I'm proud of you for that. And I'm proud of you for standin' up to that boy today."

Nancy wasn't really listening to her grandma. There were too many thoughts running through her head. She knew there was no way that she could ever go back to school and face those other kids. She didn't know how she could face anybody right now.

She stood up and ran to her room, leaving Barbara with her own thoughts about what would happen to her now. It had been a long, hard road. One that Barbara didn't want to have to travel back down. "Damn that Charlie Silver for ever coming into her daughter's life. Damn his soul forever," she thought, "for putting her family through what they had gone through. And, damn them all the day Nancy learned the whole truth."

It would be days before Nancy would finally come out of her room to set with Barbara, who seemed to be aging quickly. The toll that past events had taken on her grandma were leaving their marks. Her face and hands had more wrinkles than she cared to look at and she was getting mighty forgetful.

Nancy never went back to school and as time passed, she got to where she didn't even want to go to church or for supplies at the trading post. Every time she went out she would hear people talking. They said nasty things that she knew couldn't be true. Why she even heard two old biddies talking one day in the store and they was saying that her ma chopped her pa up with an ax and they never did find all of him. That day, she didn't even bother to tell her grandma. It was too much and her grandma wasn't doing well anyway.

For sometime now, Nancy would make little trips every now and again across the creek to Granny Silver's. It was only because, as she got older, she figured they might tell her something about her folks. But all they did was talk about how much her pa had loved her and her mommy and he would never do them no harm. They would eye one another as if trying to figure out how much they should tell her, but when she started asking questions they would just clam up.

By the time Nancy was 15, she and Barbara had moved in with Uncle Blackston. He could help take care of Barbara, as age was slipping up on her quickly. Nancy continued to hear things off and on. She was a good listener, but she didn't really have much to say in return. Sometimes she thought people must think she was deaf. Even her grandma and Blackston would whisper loud enough for her to hear. She knew in her heart that she didn't know the whole story about her folks. She also knew that she may never know, and deep down, she wasn't sure she wanted to know. Everything seemed to be a secret, and she hated secrets.

Still, it eat at her every day. She had heard so many bits and pieces of what had happened, she just couldn't put them all together. She would always believe that if her ma really did kill her pa, it was by accident. She would never believe that her own mother could have chopped her pa up with an ax and tried to burn him in the fireplace, like people said. She had seen the three graves that his pieces were supposedly buried in. Granny Silver had taken her there. She had told her there were three graves because they had found his bones in different places at three different times.

"Oh, your pa loved you," she said, as she stared at the mounds of dirt.

To Nancy, the graves didn't mean he had been cut up. He could have been buried and dug up by coyotes and scattered here and there. Seemed to her that she would spend the rest of her life wondering what really happened because no one seemed to want to tell her everything.

Then one day she was in the trading post picking up some snuff for her grandma when she overheard a couple of men folk talking around the old pot-bellied stove.

"I swear it," one man said in a loud voice. "He jumped up and said 'God save the baby.'"

"I don't believe that," another man said.

Nancy peeked around the corner to see who was talking. "Oh dear Lord," she thought, "it's Alfred Silver, her daddy's younger brother."

"Well, let me tell you this again," Alfred said, agitated because the other men didn't believe him. "Charlie come in from his liquor run. He was tired and cold so Frankie told him to lay down in front of the fireplace and take a nap. She laid the baby in his arms and he closed his eyes to go to sleep. She waited till she was sure he was sleepin', took the baby and put her to bed, then got the ax and hit him over the head. It didn't kill him right then, for he jumped up and hollered 'God save the baby,' and fell back to the floor. He was bleedin' somethin' awful, and that gal must have felt sorry for him seein' him suffer that way, so she swung the ax again and cut his head clean off."

Nancy couldn't believe what she was hearing. She had to get out of there. "How in under the sun would Alfred Silver know such a thing as that? And for him to be telling it all these years later was terrible, just terrible," she thought, as she slammed the snuff down on the counter and ran out the door.

By the time she got home, she was out of breath and crying. Uncle Blackston was sitting on the porch whittling on a stick when Nancy fell up the steps. She lay there with her head buried in her arms, wailing as if someone had just beaten her.

"What the hell is wrong with you girl?" he said rather harshly, as was the way with most men. They didn't know how to have sympathy and they sure didn't know much about teenage girls.

"Nancy," he said again. "Talk to me, girl!"

Finally, she pulled herself together. She was sick and tired of it all. She had to put it to rest. Suddenly that fierce nature of hers took control. She jumped to her feet, wiping her nose with the back of her hand.

"Uncle Blackston, I want the truth," she said matter-of-factly.

She stood right square in front of him, her hands on her boney hips, her dirty feet planted firmly on the wooden planks of the old porch. She would stand her ground this time if it was the last thing she did.

"Ma," he yelled to Barbara. "Come on out here for a spell. I thank we got some splainin' to do."

Barbara came to the door. Her faded blue dress slouched over one shoulder and she had snuff running out the corner of her mouth. She took one look at Nancy and knew she had heard something else.

She set down in the old rocking chair next to Blackston and took a deep breath, "Now what is it?" She folded her skinny arms under her sagging breasts and looked at Nancy. "Poor little girl," she thought. "She had been through so much in her young life. Why couldn't everybody just let it be?"

She listened as Nancy spilled it all out. She told them what she had heard at the trading post from Alfred. She told them all the stuff she had heard through the years from different people, stuff she had tried hard not to think about. Then she told them she was old enough to hear the truth, it didn't matter how bad it was. She needed to know, wanted to know, couldn't go on without knowing.

Barbara knew the time had come for her to answer Nancy's questions, or at least the ones she could. Truth be known, she didn't even really know herself what had happened that night all them years ago. She could only speculate, but her and Isaiah had done a lot of that back then.

"I don't really know for sure what happened Nancy," Barbara said, looking down at her wrinkled hands. "But, I'll tell you what I can.

"It was around Christmastime and I know your pa had been gone for several days. Frankie was worried somethin' furious about him. He was supposed to have been huntin' and then he was gonna stop at old man Young's and pick up some liquor. When it came out in court, they said there was a fuss, like I told you before. Frankie didn't even git to testify. Nope, she never got to tell her story atall, but she probably wouldn't of anyway. Your momma was so hush-mouthed about everything that nobody really knowed what happened that night. We don't even know, cause she was so beside herself when she finally came to the house with you, that we could never git a straight story from her. She just kept a sayin' she didn't do it. We was more concerned about keepin' her safe than hearin' what happened. We knew she didn't do it, not our little Frances. Why she weren't no bigger than a fly. She couldn't a done what they was a sayin' she did."

"The only evidence that was ever found," said Blackston, taking over where Barbara left off, "was the remains of your pa's torso, as they called it, hid in a stump. Them high-falutin' lawyers the Silvers hired tried to say your momma chopped him up with an ax and then tried to burn him in the fireplace. They said when that didn't work, she just buried the pieces here and there. But, the argument was that your momma was a little woman and there was no way she could a done all that herself."

"That's when me and Blackston was arrested for helpin' her, and the Silvers took you," Barbara said in a low voice, still looking at her trembling hands, remembering that horrible day.

Nancy sank to the floor in front of them, unable to stand any longer. Her eyes were wide with horror as her grandma and uncle continued to remember the events of that fateful time.

"Your granddaddy was off tryin' to buy seed or somethin' at that time. Cain't rightly remember now. Anyway, when he got home a couple days later and found out we was in jail, he got fightin' mad. He knowed the law pretty good and he told them that at the courthouse. They had to let me and Blackston go 'cause they had no evidence of any such thang they was a sayin'," Barbara said.

"Now, what you heard Alfred a sayin' today is somethin' that all of us have always wondered about," continued Blackston. "Just how does he know so much about that night when you and Frankie and Charlie were the only ones there, and you weren't even old enough to talk?"

"We always wondered about Alfred," Barbara said. "They put that boy on the witness stand and you wouldn't believe all the thangs he said. Had everybody confused. We know he lied about a lot a thangs. Whose to say he didn't actually do the killin' hisself? Me and Isaiah always kind of thought that, 'cause Frankie sure enough was scared a somethin'. We thought that maybe Alfred come to the house for some of that liquor Charlie picked up and, when Charlie wouldn't give it to him, they got in a fight. He was just a young feller you know, maybe 15 or so. He could a got mad and hit him with the ax. Probably didn't mean to kill him, but when he did, he got scared. Then, threatened Frankie that he would kill her, and you too, if she ever told anybody.

35

You know them Silvers are political people, but that Alfred sure is somethin' else and always has been, runnin' around shootin' his mouth off all the time. There ain't no way possible that he could know all the thangs he claims, lessen he was really there. Nobody in court wanted to accuse him of lyin' cause of his folks. I just don't know if a man could kill his own brother like that or not. But I can believe that better than I can believe Frankie done it."

"At one point," Blackston recounted, "when the trial was ended and the jury was sent out to make a decision, they come back the next day with a nine to three vote in favor of an acquittal for your momma. That tells me that even the jury, or at least most of them, didn't believe that she was guilty. They were allowed to bring the witnesses back to ask them more questions, but Frankie's lawyer weren't allowed to question them. There was stuff brought up then that wasn't even brought up in the trial and that just ain't right. There was somethin' fishy about the whole thang and the whole time, Frankie set in silence. Then, after she was sentenced to hang, seven of the jurors signed a petition to have her pardoned. But, that didn't happen either. The Silvers got what they wanted when they saw your ma hang."

"We thought maybe that's why Frankie wanted you with Jacob and Elizabeth on Ellijay 'cause that was far enough away to where Alfred couldn't get to you and try to kill you if the truth ever got out," Barbara said. "The way I see it, your momma give her life to save yours, you see what I'm a sayin' Nancy?"

"But, I still don't understand," Nancy cried. "If ma didn't really do the killin' then, why on earth is folks still sayin' she did?"

"You know how people are," Blackston answered. "When nobody really knows what happened, they go to makin' up their own stories.

You know the Silvers have their stories about what they think happened and we have ours. We just never could believe that Frankie had it in her to kill anybody on purpose. If in fact, they did get in a fuss and she thought your pa was gonna hurt her or you, then she may have hit him with somethin' that killed him, but it would have been an accident and self-defense. We just don't know.

"One thangs for certain, we shore didn't help cut him up. They never did find all of him, so whoever did do the killin', couldn't a done it by their self I don't thank. Frankie pleaded not guilty from the beginning, then they said she admitted to it in the end. But, I don't believe that. Just don't make no sense to me. Lots a folks said she didn't git a fair trial 'cause she was a woman. If she hollered self-defense, it wouldn't a mattered a bit to the men on that jury or the judge. Maybe that's why she kept her mouth shut. She knew they was gonna string her up from the beginning, whether she was guilty or not."

"I always thought that my Isaiah knew somethin' that we didn't know. But, ifen he did, he never told anybody. He fought for your mommy with everything he had in him, clear on up to the end of her life. At one point, he even thought that Zeb Cranberry had a hand in killin' your pa. A lot of folks did, but they never questioned him in court. You see Nancy, your pa was a man that lusted after all the purty girls. Everybody in this valley knowed that and everybody knowed that he had been messin' around with Cranberry's wife. Cranberry even told your granddaddy at the courthouse one day, that he was damn glad Charlie was dead and if Frankie hadn't a done it, he might have considered it hisself. Made Isaiah thank that maybe he done it and threatened our Frankie with her life, or yours, if she told. Anyway, your granddaddy never was the same after we lost our Francis and eventually, that's what killed him," Barbara said, as she got up from the rocking chair. "That reminds me, I got somethin' for you. Now's as good a time as any to give it to you."

She went in the house and came out with a folded piece of paper. Her feeble hands were trembling and she stared at it for a minute thinking about the day that Jacob had given it to her to keep for Nancy. Every day for more than a year, Barbara had unfolded the paper and stroked the hair inside. It was all that remained of her little girl and she needed it close to her. But as the years passed, she had to let go and move on with her life. Now, it was time to give it to Nancy.

"It was your mommy's," she said, handing the folded paper to Nancy. "One time, when she was in jail, your granddaddy helped her escape. She cut her pretty, long hair to look like a boy, and wore boys clothes. She was stayin' at the Erwin sisters' house and Jacob come to get her to take her back to Ellijay to be with you. They only made it to Rutherford County when they was caught. She was taken back to jail and so was Jacob and that Abe feller that came with him. Jacob told me that, before they took your ma away, she told him there was somethin' in her bag of belongings for you. That was the last time he ever got to see her, except when she was hanged."

Her voice broke for a moment and tears streamed down the creases in her cheeks. Nancy had never seen her grandma cry before, and knew this was hard for her. She never said a word as she unwrapped the paper and, for the first time that she could remember, she touched a part of her mother. She ran her fingers through the ponytail and then brought it up to her nose to smell.

"I never give it to you before because I didn't thank you was old enough," Barbara said, her voice still quivering with emotion. "But, now it's time you had it."

When Nancy went to lay the hair back into the paper, she noticed some faded writing on the old stationary. Barbara watched her granddaughter as she picked the paper up and began to read:

This dreadful dark and dismal day
Has swept my glories all a way
My sun goes down my days are past
And I must leave this world at last

Oh Lord what will become of me
I am condemned you all now see
To heaven or hell my soul must fly
All in a moment when I die

Judge Daniel has my sentence pass'd
These prison walls I leave at last
Nothing to cheer my drooping head
Until I'm numbered with the dead

But oh! That dreadful judge I fear
Shall I that awful sentence hear
Depart ye cursed down to hell
And forever there to dwell

I know that frightful ghosts I'll see
Gnawing their flesh in misery
And then and there attended be
For murder in the first degree

She looked at Barbara with the question in her eyes. "All I can figure is she must've wrote that when she was in jail or while she was at the Erwin's house. I didn't go the day they hanged her. I couldn't stand the thoughts of my baby girl a danglin' there for everyone to gawk at. Your granddaddy said she read that poem a standin' on the plank. Somebody hollered out in the crowd, 'that's a confession!' But, Frankie didn't answer them. She would take it to her grave if it was. She wasn't about to lower her head in shame. No sirree, your momma was a brave woman clear on up till the rope dropped."

Nancy held the folded paper to her heart. After all she had been through in her short life and now she finally knew why nobody liked her or wanted to be around her. None of it was her fault, but she had to take the wrath and scorn of others because of what they thought her mother did. She would be guilty for the rest of her life -- guilty of being the daughter of a murderess.

"It's best if you just put all this behind you, Nancy," Barbara was saying, but Nancy could hardly hear her. She was thinking about how her mother must have felt when they took her away from her. She was thinking about how scared her mother must have been, being accused of such a horrible thing. She was thinking of the cruel words the kids had said to her on the playground that day in fourth grade.

"Nancy, do you hear me?" Barbara said. "You got to be strong, like your mommy."

"I hear you Grandma," Nancy answered. "I will. I just need some time to thank about everythang."

Nancy took the folded paper to her room. She lay across the old quilt on her bed and studied the ponytail for a spell. Then she wrapped it back up and put it in her trunk. Like her grandmother, she would take it out every day for awhile and touch it, and smell it, trying to remember something about her. Life would go on, she knew, but from now on she vowed she would speak her mind when she heard people talking. She would not let them disgrace her or her mother ever again.

CHAPTER FIVE
1848–1850

One evening, she was sitting on the porch, just thinking like she so often did, when she saw a young feller on horseback coming toward the house. Nancy had never sparked much attention from boys in Toe River. There really weren't that many there anyway and the ones that were had always been told by their folks to stay away from her. She didn't care. Boys had always been mean to her, so why on earth would she want to have to live with one?

But Nancy was indeed becoming a young woman and she knew it. She couldn't quite put her finger on it, but something was missing. She needed somebody to put their arms around her and make her forget all the ugly things in her past -- ugly things that she had never had any control over. People were cruel to hold her accountable for what happened to her folks. She was just a baby then, how could they possibly call her a murderer? She didn't have anything to do with it. And now, here was a man riding up to her house that she had never seen before, but he had probably heard all about her.

"Evenin' ma'am," he said, tipping his hat to her. "I been on this here road for awhile and I need to take a rest. Would it be too much trouble for me to bed down here for the night?"

Nancy couldn't take her eyes off him. He wore black trousers with suspenders over a wrinkled white shirt. He was the best looking man she had ever seen. "I'll need to ask my uncle, this is his place you know," she answered as she got up from the porch to go inside and ask Blackston.

Blackston followed her back out where the young man was waiting.

"Evenin' sir," the man said. He jumped down off his horse. "As I was tellin' the young lady, I been on the road for quite a spell and me and my horse need to rest, if we could share your barn tonight. The names Parker, David Parker," he said, extending his hand.

"Well, I see no reason why you cain't sleep for the night in my barn," Blackston said, shaking the young man's hand. "I'm Blackston Stuart and this here's my niece Nancy. Go on over to the trough there and get cleaned up and we'll feed you some supper."

"Much obliged," David said. Then, he turned to look at Nancy, tipped his hat to her again and headed toward the barn.

Nancy was so excited she could hardly contain herself. She ran to her room to make sure her hair looked nice and her clothes weren't all wrinkled and … oh, she just couldn't believe that she was doing all of this over a man. What had gotten into her? But she knew what had gotten into her, and if what she had read about in the few books she had was true, then she did believe in love at first sight.

Nancy learned that David Parker was from Morganton, but had been working in Tennessee. They began a courtship that was somewhat long distance, because David could only stop in a few days at a time when he wasn't working. But he made it a point to always stop off at Nancy's anytime he was headed home and again when he was headed back to work.

Blackston grew fond of David, and even Barbara looked forward to his visits. They had never seen Nancy so happy, and that meant a lot to them. They knew she was growing up, and it wouldn't be long before she would be out on her own.

Eventually, David began sleeping in the house instead of the barn. He and Nancy spent many hours talking, holding hands and courting. In one conversation, her parents came up. Of course, word had gotten around that she was seeing some stranger and someone along the way had taken it upon themselves to stop him and warn him about her. Nancy figured it was probably one of the Silver clan, as she had come to believe they hated all of her momma's family.

Anyway, David assured her that he had grew up hearing the stories about Frankie Silver. They were horrible, yes, but he had never really believed most of them. He knew that no one really knew what had happened and he knew that regardless of all that, Nancy had been a baby at the time, so it wasn't her fault. It was just that everyone seemed to think that Nancy would grow up to be mean and evil just like her momma was. That's why no other boys had ever paid her any attention. They were afraid of her.

Nancy just thought all that nonsense was just that -- nonsense. How could anyone think her mean and evil. Damn these gossiping people. They just couldn't forget about nothin'. But, she was determined they weren't gonna get between her and her man.

For almost three years, David made his regular stops at Nancy's house, until finally the day came when he decided that he should take her for his wife. He had seen nothing bad about Nancy and from the first day he laid eyes on her, he knew that someday she would be his.

That evening while they were sitting on the porch, he took her hand in his and said, "Nancy, I been thinkin'. If it suits your grandma and your uncle, I'd like for you to marry me."

Nancy couldn't believe what she was hearing. Her heart turned a flip as she wrapped her arms around his neck. Finally, she would make a life for herself -- a better life. Of course, her life with Barbara hadn't been all that bad. But maybe now she could put everything behind her and love someone that would always take care of her and they could even raise a family.

Barbara and Blackston were almost as happy as she was. David Parker was a good man and they knew that he would take care of Nancy. And it really didn't matter if they agreed or not, Nancy was 18 years old and could do what she wanted to, and she really wanted to marry this man. So a day or two later, David and Nancy traveled to McDowell County (Morganton) and got married.

When they returned to Blackston's, Barbara had something to tell them. She had kept her word in the custody papers thus far and now she would send them off with a few pieces of furniture and an old milk cow to help them start a new home together. David's plan was to find a house or build a house for them in Morganton, but then Barbara brought out a box with some papers in it.

"When your pa was a livin', he owned property in Yancy County," she told Nancy. Her voice was low and quivery as she handed Nancy a paper. "He had inherited a hundred acres from his Uncle Will Griffith, but him and your mommy never went there. After your pa died, the land became yours, when you got up of age to get it. You're old enough now to claim it. It's only about 30 miles from here, so I figure you and David might want to build there."

Nancy really didn't know what to say as she took the land deed from her grandma's hands. She would take it to the courthouse and claim her inheritance that she didn't even know she had until now. It would be all hers; the only things she had ever owned.

Within a few days, Nancy and David made their way by wagon to the property in Yancy County. Nancy was excited as they traveled over the rough old wagon trail, pulling the milk cow behind them. Her grandma had given them the bed Nancy had slept in since she came to live with her, a table that had belonged to her mother, a rocking chair and a trunk, which now held Nancy's few belongings. She had never had much in the way of clothes and all. She had always been called "simple" -- she just never knew if that meant "simple minded" or "simple looking." She had an old hairbrush that she used to get the tangles out of her long, dark hair and she had a mirror that she could look at her likeness in, but it had a crack through the middle of it. Through the years, Barbara had hand stitched Nancy's dresses and they always seemed to be too big or too small, and the hem was always crooked. But Nancy didn't much care. When she got old enough she made her own aprons to cover the hem anyway, and she would patch her dresses till there wasn't anything left to patch. Then she would cut them into pieces and make quilts out of them. She had actually gotten pretty good at sewing and occasionally even made a few cents from the neighbors for mending their clothes or sewing them a new dress or pair of britches.

She had tried to save her money, but it always seemed something would come up and she would have to dig it out and spend it. But that didn't much matter to her either. Usually they had enough to eat, even if it was just a biscuit sopped in sorghum syrup. Nancy worked hard in the fields every year from the time she was old enough to hold a bucket or a hoe. When the crops did good they faired well through the winter months, but when the crops did poorly it could be a struggle to survive in these mountains.

Growing up that way led Nancy to believe that she would make a good wife for David. There wasn't much she couldn't do in the way of farming, tending house, or putting up food for the winter.

David looked over at Nancy and grinned. He was happy too. He was married to the prettiest little lady this side of the Smoky Mountains, and his greatest desire was to make sure she knew he felt that way. He knew Nancy had grown up poor and had been poked fun of all her life. He knew she didn't have any friends and never had nice clothes or shoes on her feet that didn't have holes in them. But all that was about to change. He would work his fingers to the bone to keep her happy.

Shortly after they passed Crabtree Church they came across an old log house on the left, across the creek. Around the house was a split rail fence that looked to have been there for quite sometime. A rooster was perched up on one of the posts watching a flock of hens peck around the red clay yard. The porch was a bit downhill from one end to the other and several strings of leather britches hung from the edge of the roof. A faint hint of smoke came from the rock chimney, but there wasn't a soul in sight.

"Best I can figure," David said, keeping the horse at a steady pace, "that house there is on our property. We best find out who it is. But first, let's go on a ways and look around."

"Sounds good to me," Nancy agreed, turning in the seat to look back at the house to see if she could see anyone.

They kept going till they were out of sight of the house and David pulled the horse to a halt.

"Well, this is it, Nancy," he said, squeezing her shoulder, as he jumped down from the wagon.

Nancy looked around, taking it all in. They owned land on both sides of Cane Branch Road -- 100 acres. For the first time in her life, Nancy felt rich. To the left was steep pasture land that went as far as the eye could see. To the right, there was a good sized field with little rolling hills covered in tiny purple wildflowers that led to the foot of the mountain. Just a short piece up, the creek ran across the road, then through a little meadow where an old shack stood, and on down alongside the foot of the mountain.

David helped Nancy out of the wagon and they walked toward the little shack. A stream ran down the side of the mountain into the creek and they followed it till it came to a head at a small spring.

"Right here is where we'll build our house," David said, hugging Nancy up against him.

"Looks like a mighty fine place to me," Nancy said with a smile on her face.

"I'm thinkin' maybe we can stay in that old shack till we get the house built, if it ain't in too bad a shape," David said as they walked hand in hand back down the mountain.

The shack was indeed in bad shape, but Nancy convinced David that it didn't matter to her, she could make a home for him anywhere. At least there was a good solid fireplace inside and a wooden shelf where they could keep the canned goods Nancy had brought with them from Barbara's. There was a stack of wood leaning against one wall and a worn out straw broom propped against the fireplace. Nancy took the broom and began getting the cobwebs out from between the logs and continued to sweep the dirt floor while David unhooked the horse from the wagon and carried in their belongings. He had brought along a rooster and a couple of good laying hens, a few tools he had, and the furniture they would need.

A short time later they stepped back and took a good, long look around at what would be their home for several months, maybe even a year, depending on the weather and how quick David could get their house raised. Winter was coming and he knew he had a lot to do before cold weather set in. At first light, he would have to get started on a shelter for the animals. He would make it small to start with and eventually they would add on to it to make a large barn. He figured he'd put it just a little piece up from the old house they had passed. That would leave room in the meadow for the cow and horse to graze, plus it was on the creek where the animals could get water.

Nancy left David to build a fire, while she rooted around in the wooden box of food items for some flour and lard to make biscuits. She cut a few slices of side meat off a slab of pork and opened a jar of peaches she and Barbara had canned. This would be their first supper in their new home.

That night, they held each other under the weight of the quilts Nancy had made. She couldn't ever remember being so happy as David tenderly took her for his own.

David had been up since first light when Nancy finally opened her eyes. It was a new day and she had plenty to do. They ate leftover biscuits and meat, and soon they were walking toward the old house they had passed the day before.

Smoke was coming out the chimney and there was a fairly old colored woman standing on the porch throwing corn out to the chickens.

"Howdy ma'am," David yelled to her from the corner of the broken fence.

The woman looked up, but never said a word. She was as big around as she was tall and her coal black hair was twisted in a bun on top of her head. Her dress near dragged the floor of the porch and she had what appeared to be snuff oozing out the corner of her mouth. She probably wasn't that old, but hard work sure had put the wrinkles in her dark brown skin. She wasn't black like the slaves that belonged to the wealthy folks. But, she wasn't as light as Nancy's Melungeon skin.

David took his hat off and asked if he could talk to the man of the house.

"Ain't no man of the house round here," she said. "You gots some'in to say, you says it to me."

"The names David Parker and this heres my wife Nancy. Seems your livin' on our land we just claimed and I was wonderin' how you come to be here."

The woman studied Nancy for a minute, then she dropped the pan and came toward them. "Oh my Lord Jesus in heaven child. You be that Nancy Silver from over yonder in Toe River." She took Nancy by the hand and led her toward the house.

Nancy was startled at first. She knew what was coming and she had hoped to get away from it all out here. But, it wasn't to be.

"Your daddy be Charlie -- po' old Charlie Silver," she said, shaking her head. "I's sorry. I gets a little carried away sometime and ferget my manners." She held her hand out to David, "I's Sinda Griffith. Her pappy's uncle, Mr. Will, was my daddy."

Sinda looked at Nancy and seen the question in her eyes. "Here, set fer a spell and I's tell you all about it."

51

David leaned against a porch post and Nancy sat down in an old chair, the woven bottom tattered with age.

"My mammy was a slave to Mr. Will fer years on end. Yes sir, she wuz," Sinda began. "She sure enough wuz a purty thang and that Mr. Will took a likin' to her. And, she took a likin' to him, too. Ain't no secret in these parts fer masters to take slaves fer their own. Even theys wives knows it. Don't pay no never mind though. Jest saves them from haven to spread them purty white legs," she grinned real big and Nancy noticed half her teeth were missing.

"Anyhows, that be when I wuz borned. Weren't allowed to call him Pappy, no sirree, he always be Mr. Will to me, even though he wuz my pappy." She walked to the edge of the porch, spit her snuff out and kept on talking.

"When Mr. Will died, he left freedom papers for Mammy and me. Said we wuz to live in this here house he had built just for her. This be where they do all their lovemakin' you see," she laughed and slapped her knee.

Nancy couldn't help but laugh, too. Sinda was such a jolly soul, the likes of which Nancy had never seen before, and it made her feel good.

"Anyway, papers said we could live here till we died and Mammy been dead a while now. But I's still a kickin'. Don't aim to go no where, lesson youns run me off."

"Now, Miss Sinda, we ain't got no intentions of doin' that," David said.

"Call me Aunt Sinda," she interrupted. "That's how folks 'round these parts know me."

"Ok, Aunt Sinda," David said, smiling. "So long as we know you belong here, you can stay. We aim to build a house on that mountain over there and a barn just up from you a piece. If you need anything, we'll be stayin' in the little shack for now."

"Reckon I don't needs a thang. Been doin' fine by my lonesome fer a good spell now. Just happy to have some neighbors close enough to holler at now and again. Spect there'll be some little uns comin' along soon," she grinned at Nancy, whose face was beginning to turn a pale shade of red. "That be fine missy. Aunt Sinda loves them younguns. Now youns git on outa here, I's got work to do," she said, shuffling Nancy toward the yard.

"It's nice to meet you Aunt Sinda," Nancy turned and said. "I'll be seein' you soon."

"You too child," Sinda said.

"That be Charlie's po' little girl, right here on Cane Branch," she muttered to herself as she walked back toward the house. "Po' little Nancy. Po' old Charlie."

"I like that old woman," Nancy said, skipping up the middle of the road. "It'll be nice to have her around and she didn't even make no mention of my momma."

"That's good," David said. "I think we're gonna be very happy here."

CHAPTER SIX
1851–1862

Nancy and David loved living on Cane Branch. David built their house right on the side of the mountain, close to the spring, and before long they left the little shack. There was so much to do, but finally they had a huge barn, large fields of corn and cane, a few fruit trees and even several head of cattle. They faired well in Yancey County and in September of 1852 Jacob William "Bill" Parker was born.

Nancy named her first born after Jacob Stuart, the man who fathered her almost from the day her real father died until she went to live with Grandma Stuart when she was five.

True to her word, Aunt Sinda would make trips up the mountain to help Nancy out all she could. In return, they made sure she had plenty to eat. For the first time in her life, Nancy had made a friend with Sinda. It felt good for her to have someone to talk to and Sinda never mentioned one thing about Charlie Silver to her again.

Sunday mornings David and Nancy would get up and go to Crabtree church, where they eventually met all their neighbors. There was Greenberry Silver, a first cousin to Charlie, and his wife, Malinda. Greenberry had also inherited 100 acres of land from Uncle Will. His land butted right up against David and Nancy's. Greenberry was polite to them, but Nancy always wondered, in the back of her mind, if they were just being neighborly. They all knew the stories -- they, the Silvers, had theirs and she had hers.

There was also Silas McCurry. He was a farmer that lived on up the road in the holler. Silas and his wife, Hanah, came to visit David and Nancy often or would walk home with them from church for a good Sunday eating.

William A. Willson became good friends with David and would often help out on the farm.

There were plenty of good families that lived on Cane Branch and they were all good about helping each other out. Nancy found herself amongst many friends through the next several years, which was something new to her. For David, it was easy to make friends. He was such a respectful man. Everyone who knew anything of him called him friend. He believed in doing the right thing at all times and he was quick to reprimand Nancy when her mean streak would get the best of her. He had a reputation to uphold and he expected her to do the same. But she sure could be a feisty little thing; that was one of the reasons David fell in love with her to begin with.

When little Bill was just two years old, Nancy gave birth to Charles Wesley, September of 1854. Nancy named little Charles after her father. It was the least she felt she could do, considering that she never knew him.

Every two or three years, Nancy and David had another child.

Retta Elizabeth was born April, 1857. Nancy named her after Elizabeth Stuart, who had mothered her until Grandma Stuart took her.

Margaret Alice was born February of 1859 and was named after David's sister, Margaret.

Mary Elmira "Myrah" was born March of 1861. She was named after David's sister Mary.

Things had gone well for David and Nancy on Cane Branch, even though winter months were a bit tough. They farmed the land and gathered in food to do for bad weather. Even the boys, when they were old enough to carry a bucket, would go to the fields to help David plant, work, and harvest. Nancy and the girls did the washing and the cleaning, putting up food, drying apples and peaches, and sewing their clothes and quilts. These had been the happiest years of Nancy's life.

The year before Myrah was born, word had come to the cove that a Mr. Abraham Lincoln was running for president. David knew that if he was elected that taxes would be going up for the South, and they were already paying more than the North. South Carolina had already said they would leave the United States and form their own nation if their taxes went up. David and most of the neighbor men figured that if Lincoln was indeed elected, there would be a war between the states because the South wasn't about to give up their rights without a fight.

They were all willing to go to war if it came to that, and Nancy and the other women were worried about being left alone.

"I can assure you dear lady," David told Nancy, "that if war breaks out and I leave you and the children here, it will be tough on you, but I know you'll be alright. It's just what we have to do."

As months passed, more and more talk of war came to the cove. Lincoln was indeed elected President and David and the other men knew that it was just a matter of time.

David watched Nancy nursing their newborn, Myra, and he couldn't help but wonder what would happen to them while he was away. It was hard enough on her with him around, how on earth could he leave her, with all these children, to farm the land, tend the cattle and take care of themselves?

Nancy looked up and saw him watching her. "What's on your mind?" she asked.

"I was just thinkin' about how hard it will be on you when I have to leave. Greenberry says it may be within the year. If William don't leave when I do, he has agreed to help git the fields planted and anything else you need that he can do. He's a good feller and I know we can trust him. I know Aunt Sinda will help you take care of the children. And, I was just thinkin' that, maybe, we could get my brother Elijah and his wife, Mary, to move into the little shack. Last time I heard from him, he was wantin' to move out this way with us. Said we could sure help each other out if him and Mary lived here and we could share the farmin' and such. Seein' as how you just had a baby, I figure Mary could be of big help to you, too."

Nancy thought that was a good idea, though she didn't really know Mary too well. But that didn't matter much, what mattered was that they could help each other. Before long, David rode into Morganton to bring Lige and Mary back to Cane Branch. It was just in good time too, for war had broke out in the states. The first shots reported had been in South Carolina. Other reports were coming from up in Virginia.

Every day that passed, Nancy and David knew could be their last together. David busied himself with getting the farming done, mending fences and anything else he could do to insure that, when he did leave, his farm would be in good standing.

Once the harvest came in, Nancy and Mary put up everything they could get their hands on. They worked from sun up to sun down making syrup, stringing beans, burying cabbage and turnips, drying fruit and filling the cellar David had dug in the bank behind the house with dried beans, extra meal and coffee. They would go to church on

Sundays and pray that their men wouldn't have to leave, that maybe God could spare them from this awful war.

For the most part, Nancy and Mary got along pretty good. Mary sometimes got on Nancy's nerves when she would start talking about some of the women in the cove. Sometimes, Mary just thought she was so perfect. But, Nancy kept her mouth shut, knowing that David would never forgive her if she ever hurt his sister-in-law's feelings.

Usually when Mary started her bantering, Nancy would put the baby on her back in a blanket sling like Aunt Sinda had taught her, and go into the fields with David to hoe corn or pick beans, just whatever he needed her to do.

When cold weather commenced on them, usually around Thanksgiving, the entire neighborhood gathered at each farm for hog killings. They would shoot the hogs and gut them, then build a big fire under a huge, black kettle of water. When it started boiling, they would dip the hog in the water to loosen its hair. Then they would lift it out of the water and scrape it, until all the hair was gone. They would cut up the meat and cook the liver, kidneys, tongue and other small pieces to make pudding. They would grind these parts up and season it with salt and pepper. Then the women would thicken the broth with cornmeal, cook and stir it awhile, put it in the ground up meat and put it in pans. When it cooled, it could be sliced and fried until it was golden brown on both sides. Then they would pour syrup over it for a delicious meal. The pudding would keep all winter, covered with about a half inch of lard and kept in the cellar. The rest of the meat was hung in the smoke house and cured. The men wanted as much meat as they could keep without spoiling to tide the womenfolk and children over until such time as they returned home. It was inevitable now, that soon, there wouldn't be a single man left in the cove -- they would all be off fighting the war.

David was worried about Nancy, but maybe not as much as some of the other men were about their wives. Nancy had come up in a hard way. It wasn't unusual for her to work alongside the men folk. She had helped Blackston in the fields when she was barely old enough to carry a hoe. She had done all her own sewing and mending for years and Grandma Stuart had taught her all there was to know about putting up food for the winter. Nancy could chop wood and build a fire as good as any man, and she even knew how to handle the old shotgun that hung above the fireplace. David had taught her that himself.

It was before their first son was born, when David was building the house. He hadn't anticipated his closest neighbor being a panther. One day he and Nancy were chopping away at an old hickory tree when David caught a glimpse of something black sneaking through the laurel thicket. He caught Nancy by the arm and whispered for her to quit swinging the ax and, ever so slowly, start backing down the mountain. She started to question him until she seen a fear in his eyes she had never seen before. She dropped the ax to her side and David began to lead her backwards down the side of the mountain, never taking his eyes off the cat.

He knew from stories he had heard tell, that a panther stalked its prey. He knew if they sped up the panther would speed up and pounce on them first chance it got. Weren't no telling how long that thing had been watching them, just waiting.

Nancy followed David's eyes to the thicket. When she saw the large, black panther, it took everything she had in her not to break lose from David and run for the shack. But she knew better. Grandma Stuart had told her one time about her sister's boy getting mauled by one of these mountain cats. Said it didn't kill him, but it left him scarred for life. He was playing in the edge of the woods when the cat pounced on him, his long, sharp claws digging into the boys face. His pa heard him, or the panther one, scream and ran out the back door with his gun. Said it was the biggest panther ever seen in these parts. "Poor little boy," Grandma said, "would a been better off dead, the way that painter left him." Now wasn't a good time for Nancy to be thinking such things, but she trembled at the memory.

David hadn't thought to bring his gun with him that morning, and now he was sorry he hadn't. He held onto Nancy as tight as he could, all the while watching the panther. When it finally came out of the laurel, it crept up on an old fallen tree and lay down at the end of it, looking down on them as they crept, ever so slightly, down the mountainside. Nancy glanced over her shoulder and could see the little shack.

"We're almost there," she whispered.

The cat continued to eye them from his perch on the old tree. David knew he was patiently waiting for the big lunge. So they would stop, then they would take several slow steps backwards. They would stop, then start again, trying to confuse the animal. This worked for a short time, then the cat began to fidget. Then, he crouched down and tucked his head between his two front paws. Just as the cat jumped, David hollered for Nancy to run.

Nancy had never ran so hard in her life. Neither of them looked back, but instinct told them both that he was right on their heels. Nancy could almost feel that thing breathing down the nape of her neck, it was so close.

Finally, they reached the back door of the shack and, as they fell inside, the panther lunged again. Only this time, David had the door shut. He and Nancy were leaning against it when the thump of the panther hit the outside of it, nearly knocking them over. David managed to get the board locked in place across the door, then ran to get his shotgun. By the time he snuck back outside from around front, there was no sign of the panther.

"Ever shot a gun before Nancy?" he asked her, all out of breath from their near escape.

"Nope," she said. "But I aim to learn now."

"And I reckon I'll be the one to teach you," he said, holding her close to him.

His stupidity had darn near cost them their lives that day, and he meant for it to never happen again.

Now he was glad he had taught Nancy how to handle the old shotgun. They never seen the panther after that but figured, on occasion, he had come back and swiped a chicken or two from the yard. David knew if Nancy ever did see him again she would kill him, or anything else for that matter, that threatened to get between her and the children. This was a relief for him, now that he knew he would be leaving her soon. The gun would be her only protection while he was gone.

Sometimes bad things happen for a good reason. He figured that's what made that old panther get after them that day. If it hadn't been for that, he would probably have never thought to teach Nancy to shoot. Since then, she had killed more squirrels than he had, and they sure tasted good stewed in a pot with vegetables. That little woman of his sure could cook. He supposed that would be one of the biggest things he would miss about being at home if he had to leave.

Since the start of the war, North Carolina had not decided whether to join in the cause or not. They didn't want to be a part of the Union. But they didn't want to join the South either. They wanted to remain neutral. But realized that the state was going to be involved whether they fought or not. So North Carolina men began volunteering for duty.

The only thing required to be a captain in the war was to get 100 or more men to follow you, and James McDowell didn't think that would be a problem at all. McDowell was a good, honest man, and he felt like he could lead a troop of men into war and make a difference. He was a North Carolina man himself, born and raised in these mountains. He knew that other men raised here would make good soldiers.

McDowell made his way through Morganton into Yancy County, putting the word out that he needed volunteers. When the men in Cane Branch got wind of it, they gathered at the church for a meeting. Some of them decided to volunteer and some decided to stay in the valley and help the womenfolk out. They all knew that, whether they volunteered or not, if the war lasted any time at all, they would be made to join by the government.

David was one of the first to say that he would go. He was a political man in his own right, but he was also a farmer and he knew that he had to do all he could to save what he had worked so hard for. He didn't want to leave his family, none of them did. David, however, felt like he was in as good a position to leave as any of them, plus, he had a wife that he knew could take care of things while he was gone. He had his house in order and his fields harvested and put up. Nancy and the children would have plenty to eat for a while and, even though little Myra was only one year old, Mary and Aunt Sinda could help with her and the others. If need be, he could even move Nancy Carrell in the house with them.

Nancy Carrell was a friend of Nancy's she had met at church. Miss Carrell was the same age as Nancy, had never been married and was still living with her folks on the other side of Greenberry's property. She would often come and stay with them to help take care of the kids while Nancy worked with David in the fields. She had mentioned several times that she would love to get out on her own. David couldn't pay her anything right now for staying with Nancy, but he was sure that when he returned home from the war he could give her a little compensation for her time.

When David got home that evening Nancy was sitting in the rocking chair, her hands folded in her lap. She had been sitting there just thinking, knowing that her greatest fear was about to happen.

"I'm sorry, Nancy," David said, laying his hand on her shoulder. "But, you know it's the right thang to do."

Nancy jerked away from his touch. She was fighting hard to hold back the tears that threatened to roll down her cheeks.

"No, David," she spat at him. "The right thang to do is to take care of me and the younguns. The right thang to do is git the seed in the ground come spring so we don't starve to death. The right damn thang to do is not to leave me atall!"

By now, she was standing up, feet planted firmly on the plank floor, hands on her hips -- my Lord, she was mad. David had seen her like this before. When they built their house, Nancy had wanted it closer to the foot of the mountain. David had tried to explain to her that it would be better where he wanted it, because it was closer to the spring and a little more out of sight of the road. But Nancy didn't want to have to trudge up and down that mountain every time she went somewhere. David stood his ground though, he had to let Nancy know that he wore the pants in the house. It sure was hard changing her mind, once Nancy got something in her head. He knew he would have as hard a time as ever convincing her of all the reasons he had to go to war, while all she could think about was all the reasons he should stay.

"Now don't git mad, Nancy," he said to her in a quiet, calm voice, which was his way.

Damn, she hated him when he talked to her like that. She didn't want him to leave. She didn't want to be alone. But she knew that what he was saying was true. He could either go now voluntarily or he could wait till they called on him. Either way, he would be leaving her.

David watched the anger fade from Nancy's eyes and tears spill over instead. He reached for her and she ran into his arms. She buried her face against his strong, hard chest and cried till her whole body shook. David ran his hand through the back of Nancy's long, dark hair and breathed in the scent of her body. He was a man through and through, but right now, it was hard for even him to hold back his emotions. He closed his eyes and wondered if he would ever hold her like this again once he was gone. Would he ever get to come back home and smell the sweet scent of her golden skin? Right now, at this very moment, he wanted to make wild, passionate love to her, like he had never done before. He wanted to savor every crevice of her neck, her breasts, her thighs, so that he could take that memory with him into battle. It would be these memories of her that would keep him alive. It would be these memories that he hoped would bring him home.

CHAPTER SEVEN
1862

On March 21 David and Elijah enlisted in Co. B 54 Regiment.

July 1, 1862

Camp Johnson near Kinston

Dear wife and children it is through the mersies of god that I am permitted to seat myself in order to drop you a few lines. I can say to you that my health is tolerable good this morning. I arrived at this plaise on yestardy about one oclock in the afternoon and found all the Boys well except Wm. J. Thomas. He was complaining with his head acheing though he is better to day.

I will now gave you the details of my Journey from my father to this plaise. I arrived at granfathers on Thursday about sun set, tired nearly down. I don't think that I could a went one mile futher. I then got uncle Peter epley to take me to the head of the Road. I got thare about half an hour before the cars come up.

I took the cars for Salisbury. I arrived thare about sun set. Stayed thare till nine oclock. I then took the cars for Raleigh road. All night slept none. The cars was so full that all the men that was on board could not get seats. Thare was seven cars with about sixty men in a car. It was so heavy loaded that just eleven miles above Raleigh she stald. The engineered worked about one hour a trying to get up the graid, but failed. He then had to cut of some of the cars and run them about two miles ahead to a switch off and leave them. He then come back and got the rest and took them on to the rest and hitched them to gether and struck out for Raleigh.

We arrived at Raleigh about nine oclock in the morning. I then had to get off of the cars and go up in town to get transpotation to Kinston or pay three dollars and go on so I thought it best to wait till five oclock in the eavening. So I then concluded to go and hunt up Wm Hutchins or see if he was dead. So I went to the fair ground ospital and to my supprise the first ospital I entered thare Wm Hutchins stared me in the faise, for the first man in the ospital I walked in gave him my hand he seamed mity glad to see me. I stayed with him about two hours. He was on the mend as fast as a man could be. He looks nearly as well as ever he did though he is weak yet. The feaver settled in one of his hips and it hurts him right smart. It is swelled smartly. He told me that he would be at home in a week or two. He said he thought if he improved on as he had for the last week that he would be able shortly.

I then went back to town to hunt the transportation office. I found it and got transportation to my regiment. Let it be whare it might it was reported in Raleigh that my regiment had gone to Petersburg va. So if it had gone thare it would cost me nothing to went to them. I then took the cars at five oclock in the evening and went down to Goldsboro 50 miles. Got thare awhile after dark.

68

I have not spaise here to tell it all. Plase direct you letter to Kinston in care capt. Kibler 54 Regiment NC troops so I shall have to close by saying farewell.

David Parker to his Wife

Little Myra was just one year old when David left to fight in the Civil War. As he walked out the door that cool March morning, Nancy and the children stood in the yard to bid him farewell. Ten-year-old Bill promised his daddy that he would try his best to be the man of the house.

"I promise Pa, I'll watch over Ma and the rest of 'em," he said, as he shook his father's hand. "Don't you worry none, you jest git in thare and kill us a Yankee."

"Yeah, kill us a Yankee Pa," eight-year-old Charlie echoed behind his brother, pretending to shoot a gun.

"You boys don't be talkin' like that," Nancy scolded. "Your pa ain't gonna kill nobody lessen he ain't got no choice."

Retta clung to David's britches with one hand, her thumb stuck in her mouth with the other. She was too young to know where he was going -- all she knew was that he was leaving and she didn't want him to go.

Nancy stood holding Myra, while Margaret Alice hid in her skirts.

He did look handsome, Nancy thought, as she looked at David in the new britches she had just sewed him, a white shirt with buttons up the front and black suspenders. He reminded her of that first day she had seen him riding up to the porch at Grandma Stuarts. Dang if that man still didn't make her heart turn flips.

"Promise you'll write me at least once a week," he said, tilting her chin up so she would be looking him in the eyes.

"I promise," she whispered.

"Them letters is what's gonna keep me goin' and I need to always know that you and the children are alright. I can help you with the money I left you, too, so you know when and what to spend it on. Just remember to be stingy with what food you have. It ain't gonna last forever, but hopefully it will do you till I get back."

He hugged her long and hard against him, kissed her lips, and he was gone. Just like that. Nancy and the children watched as he walked down the steep slope to the bottom of the mountain. He turned around and waved, engraving the image of his family in his mind, then he headed off down the road.

For several moments, Nancy just stood there silent. Then, she heard a whimper between her skirts. "My pa weaven me," three-year-old Margaret Alice cried.

Nancy stooped and hugged her close. She wanted to cry too, but knew that she had to be strong for the younguns.

"It's ok Ma," Bill said, laying his hand on her shoulder. "I'll be takin' care of youns."

"I know you will," Nancy said, as she stood up. "Now, go on. Be off with all of youns. We got work to do." She wiped her nose with the back of her hand and stood straight, showing the strength that she always mustered up inside of her. No way would her children ever think she was weak, no sirree.

Aunt Sinda was on the porch when she seen David come around the bend. "Well, I'll be," she called out to him. "So's you off to fight in that thare war that's a goin on, are ya?"

"Reckon, I am Aunt Sinda," David said, tipping his hat to her. "You help Nancy take care of them children now, you hear, and I'll make sure you get somethin', for it when I git home."

"Oh, I will Mister David. Don't you worry non 'bout them. You jest bring yerself back home in one piece. Don't you go gettin' killed by none a them dadjim Yankee men. Yous is a whole lot biggeren them. Smarter too, I's reckon."

David kept walking, "I'll be back soon."

"I's shore do hope so Mister David. I's shore do hope so."

In his heart, David truly believed he would be returning soon. There was no way he could figure that the war would last long.

May the 4, 1862

Camp mangum near Raleigh

Dear wife and children. I now seat my self in order to drop you a few lines. I can inform you that I am well at this time and all the rest of the boys is well. I can inform you that we had a tiresome journey before we reached this plaise. We taken the car a Friday at one oclock and reached Raleigh next morning by sun up. We then struck to camp Mangum 4 mile back on the rail road and put up our tents. We have bread and meat a plenty. Thare was three redgiments left her yesterday and thare has to leave three redgiments to day going to golds barough. We were the first company here to ward another redgiment. Thare is but two company here to ward redgiment a bout two hour after we got in camps thare come in another company from comberland county NC.

We are looking for two companys here to day from wilks county. We past them at Salbery. I can in form you that my back is on the mend. I have not had many pains since I left home. I have had my health ever since I left home. We have good officers I think. Nothing more at preasant, your true husband till Death. You must Direct you letter to Raleigh.

While writing thare has come in three company which makes five companys here now. So I will close by saying fare well as for now. I have not heard scarcy a word since I left home.

I want you to hire some body else to do your plowing if William Wilson does not do it and do not stand on the price for I tell you that thare will not be much corn made this side Morganton for I tell you that it is the poorer country that I ever seen in all my life. People is not done planting corn here yet. There is lots of people along the rail road some just braking up there corn ground. So I shall have to come to a close by saying fare well.

David Parker to his Wife

Nancy had kept her word and wrote to David every week. The only problem was getting the letters to him. He had left her money for stamps and she would send them to the post office in Burnsville with first one and then another of her neighbors. Several times she had even harnessed up the old horse and took them herself, leaving Aunt Sinda to tend the kids. But once they were in the mail bag she didn't know where they went. She just figured that one day they would all find a way to David and he would have a whole bunch of letters at one time. So she just kept writing.

Here it was May already and she was trying to get her corn in the ground. True to his word, William had done the plowing for her, but he had his own farm to tend, so he left the planting up to her and Mary. She sure hoped her crop did well this year. The way David talked in his letter, she would be able to sale a lot of it if she didn't have to put it all up to feed them and the farm animals.

May the 8, 1862
Camp mangum near Raleigh

Nancy, I want you to send me a long letter and send it by Wm Hutchins and tell me how you are getting a long with your farming. Give me all the news in Yancy concerning the war. I can inform you that I have write you one letter before this. It will reach Burnville by Friday. Nancy I want you to compose yourself as well as you can for I don't think it will be long till I shall see you again for I think the war will seas before long and then I can come home to stay with all the time. I want you not to studdy about me for I am at home here. We have a fine company. Nancy I want you to make all the corn you can for I tell you that is nothing making down here. Hire anybody you can and do not stand on the price. If you have not got your corn planted, plant on till you get it planted for there is no time lost yet if is as cold in yancy according as it is here.

David Parker to his wife Nancy Parker

Nancy read the latest letter with great interest. Her eyes brightened when she heard that her David might be coming home soon. He hadn't even been gone two months, but already she felt the weight of the world on her shoulders. Not only was she lonely, but there was just too much for her to do, and take care of the children too. Poor little Bill had done his best to take over David's part of the work. He milked the cow, gathered the eggs, chopped wood, took the old shotgun hunting and even helped plow some of the field. He was so tired by nightfall that he could barely make it through supper without falling asleep.

"Bill, you got to quit workin' so darn hard and take time to play ever now and again," Nancy would tell him often.

"Cain't Ma," Bill would say. "I promised Pa I'd help and I'm helpin' as best I can."

"But, you cain't do it all."

"Ain't doin' it all, just what I can, that's all."

Try as she may, she couldn't get him to understand. He wanted to be a man and he was becoming one way before his time.

There were still a few men left in the valley and she still had a little money, so Nancy decided that maybe it was time for her to try and hire somebody else to help her. Then Bill could get back to doing the things boys his age did.

When Nancy got David's next letter, she was glad to hear that he was doing well and had already started making some extra money. He was cooking for 15 of the Yancy County boys for one dollar a month for each man. That sure would help Nancy out. At the bottom of the letter, Nancy was surprised to see a few lines written for Nancy Carrell. In them, David was asking Ms. Carrell to stay with her and the children and help out as much as she could. He even said that he would pay her when he returned home if she would do this for him.

"I reckon he thanks I cain't take care a myself," Nancy said the next day, as she handed the letter to Nancy Carrell to read.

"Oh, I would love to stay with you Nancy," she said. "I'll pack my belongings and be there this afternoon sometime."

Nancy wasn't sure if she liked the idea of Nancy Carrell sharing her house or not. But David had thought it through, and he thought it would help her out. And, she had to admit, she could use the help. At least Miss Carrell was her friend and he hadn't asked some of them other old biddies that talked behind her back.

It never ceased to amaze Nancy that folks could go to church and let on to be such fine Christians, and all the while they're sitting in the pews talking bad about folks. She kept her ears open and heard all the gossip. She knew that William K. Robinson ran a bootlegging operation back in the holler somewhere, and she knew that old man Hensley liked pretty young women like herself. She also knew that his wife knew it, but would never admit to it. There wasn't anything she could do about it no how. Women folk had no rights. They were just there to do the cooking, cleaning and childbearing. Other than that, they had no say in nothing. Sometimes it just made her fighting mad, then David would have to step in and quieten her down. He had never raised a hand to her, she was thankful for that. But he sure did have a way of shutting her up, just by telling her to.

Now Elijah was a little more stern with Mary. But Mary wasn't like Nancy. She was quiet and a bit timid. She never stood up for herself and just let folks run all over her. Then Nancy Carrell had to come in and start running her mouth. Said she had overheard Elijah telling her pa one day that David ought to put a stop to Nancy speaking her mind out in public. It was bad enough where she came from and folks might start saying David was afraid to shut her up, afraid she might do to him what her ma did to her pa.

Those words cut Nancy clean through when she heard them and that's what she told David in her next letter. Course he got that letter and went straight to Elijah and confronted him. He had the nerve to write Nancy back and ask her to send Lige a letter because he said he did not say what she heard he said. That really added fuel to the fire. No way was Nancy going to write that man a letter. David could believe what he wanted to. She would get to the bottom of this herself.

Nancy was out of breath by the time she got to the little shack at the foot of the mountain. Mary was outside doing her wash in the big black iron pot over the fire when she saw Nancy come stomping through the yard.

"What's ailin' you Nancy?" Mary asked, wiping the sweat off her brow with the back of her hand. She could tell Nancy was mad about something and she just hated it when she got this way.

"Ailin' me?" she scorned, throwing the letter toward Mary. "I'll tell you what's ailin' me. That damn husband of yours, that's what's ailin' me. Now David 'spects me to write Lige a letter apologizin' I reckon."

"Apologizin' for what?" Mary asked, drying her hands on her apron so she could read the letter.

Nancy told her what Nancy Carrell had overheard Elijah saying to her pa. There was no reason for her to think it was made up. Nancy Carrell was her friend, she wouldn't make up a lie like that. But Mary believed otherwise.

"Nancy," she said in her little squeaky voice that drove Nancy crazy, "you know my Lige would never say anything to hurt you. Why he's always liked you. Says you've made a good wife for his brother. Never heard nothin' from him 'bout where you come from."

"What's that supposed to mean?" Nancy asked. She now had her hands on her skinny little hips and Mary thought for a second that Nancy just might punch her. She took a step back and held her hands out in front of her.

"Now hold on a minute Nancy. There ain't no use in you gettin' all fired up over nothin'. You're the one that said it, not me. I don't care where you come from and I dang shore ain't gonna fight you over it. Best thang for you to do is march right back up that there mountain and tell Miss Carrell that she best keep her mouth shut. This ain't no time for us to be bickerin' with one another."

"Well, if that didn't beat all. Little miss perfect actually did have some spunk in her," Nancy thought as she lifted her skirts and stomped back up the mountain.

Nancy knew Mary was right. This wasn't the time for them to be fussing at one another. The women in the valley had to stick together while the men were away. All they had was each other.

Now that she had calmed down a little, there was something else in David's letter that had struck a chord with Nancy. He had said that Silas had the measles. Dear Lord, she sure hoped her David didn't get them. Worse yet, what if that dreaded disease made its way to Cane Branch? They could all die without the war ever claiming a single one of them.

Nancy had put in a good stand of corn, but she knew she would never be able to harvest it herself. She would have to get William to help her. Her money was getting scarce, but David had sent word to William that if she couldn't pay him, he would as soon as he got home.

David and Elijah stayed in Raleigh until July. David did get the measles, but faired well through them as did most all the men in his camp. They had plenty to eat -- cornbread, bacon, peas, wheat bread and rice -- that enabled them to keep their strength up. There had been no deaths in their company, though things seemed to be heating up a bit. In July, David's regiment moved to Camp Johnson near Kingston. Then the first of August, they moved to Camp Campbell. David wasn't seeing much fighting where he was, but was anticipating going up into Richmond, Va.

Once again, Nancy's letters weren't getting to David. The mail was slow getting into the camps mainly because they moved around a lot. David tried to keep Nancy informed of where to send his letters. He wanted to know everything that was going on with her and the children. Even though he wasn't there, he was still the man of the house and he had to make sure that everything was done properly. David still had not got any monthly wages and wasn't sure when, or if, he ever would. So he started scouting around the camps for horse bones and saddle leather. From these, he made bone rings and breast pins for the men to send home to their womenfolk. He would keep part of the money he made from the jewelry and get the rest to Nancy.

Come September, David's regiment was in Richmond. It was the likes of which David had never seen.

"I saw whare they had several fights. I saw several hundred graves and the yankeys ware just covered whare they lay on the ground just a little earth throwed upon the boddy and some of their legs and arms and heads was missin. I saw some of there shoes with there feet in them. Their feet had come off at there ankles. I saw some of their heads lying thare, they would kick them about like gourdes. Our men

was buried wright. The timber was cut all to pieces with
cannon balls and bullets. I can't see how anybody escaped
alive though I did not get to whare the main fight was,"

he wrote Nancy in one letter.

In the same letter, he told her about how everything up North had been destroyed and he didn't know how long they would be there.

Nancy was beside herself with worry. She wished so badly that David could come home to her and the children. She missed him terribly. At night, she would cry herself to sleep. She couldn't let the children see, for she was their strength now. They would often ask when their pa was coming home. She would tell them "soon." That's all she knowed to say to them.

By the end of September, Nancy was out of money. David wrote and told her that he had made seven dollars and 25 cents from his jewelry that week and would send some of the money to her, along with a likeness of him, in a letter to his uncle. She sure was glad to hear that he would be sending her money and stamps, but she was even happier to be getting a photograph of him.

Since Nancy had the argument with Mary, she had not seen much of her. Mary had not offered to help her in the garden, so when vegetables started coming in, Nancy gathered them up for her own family. After awhile, she got to feeling sorry for Mary's two younguns, so she picked them a basket of vegetables out of the garden and left it on the porch.

Several times she had tried to talk to Mary. She wasn't about to apologize, for she didn't think she had done anything wrong. But darn it, they needed each other right now and she knew David would be fighting mad at her if he thought she had done something to make Mary mad.

Then, she got to thinking, if Mary was going to make David think that anyway, she might just ought to give her something to really be mad about.

No, she couldn't do that. But she sure enough started thinking out loud to Nancy Carrell and Nancy Carrell seemed to be enjoying all the uproar, while Aunt Sinda was quick to tell Nancy that she just best leave it alone. But try as she might, Nancy couldn't just leave it alone. She was out of money, the kids needed clothes and shoes before winter set in, she was working her fingers to the bone trying to keep up with the garden and the cooking and the cleaning and caring for the children, and all the while little miss perfect Mary sat down there, all smug in the cabin that she and David had let them live in, never offering to lift a finger to help her in any way.

Nancy stewed about all these things for days. The more she thought about it, the madder she got. She felt sure that Lige had said the things Nancy Carrell had said he said and Mary was just covering up for him. Heck, Mary probably felt the same way about her. She felt sure that was the reason Lige wanted to come here to begin with, to protect David from her. They were against her from the beginning and out to destroy the only happiness she had ever had in her life. She'd be damned to hell if she was going to let that happen.

Aunt Sinda came in to give Nancy a hand with stringing beans and said she had seen Mary in the garden. "I's stopped fer a spell and jest asked how she was a fairin'. She's lookin' a might scrawny to me. Anyhows, she says she be takin' the younguns to see her ma fer the night and needed a few vegetables to carry along. I's tried to talk to her 'bout helpin' you out a little more, but she wanted to hear nothin' 'bout you or anything else fer that matter. I jest don't knows 'bout her," Sinda said, as she filled her lap with green beans.

"Well," Nancy Carrell chimed in, bouncing Myra on her knees, "I don't know about her either. Nancy, you sure enough stirred somethin' up in that woman when you jumped on her about Elijah. She don't like you one little bit anymore. But, thang is, she ain't got nowhere to go, so she about has to stay in the shack. Seems to me, she oughta be thinkin' about that instead a stirrin' up trouble."

That night Nancy lay in bed thinking about all these things until she couldn't lay there any longer. She climbed out of bed, lit the oil lamp and headed down the mountain. There was a rage brewing in her like she had never felt before. She was sure it had something to do with her momma, but she couldn't quite put her finger on it. She just figured it was all the years she had been made fun of and pointed at and talked about. It was all the years she had been scared of what people thought that made her find that evil place in her heart that had been hidden there, just waiting for the right time to come out. That would be tonight.

She went in the shack through the back door, holding the lamp low so anyone who might be passing through wouldn't see it's glow. At the foot of the bed, she opened Mary's trunk where she found several yards of homemade cloth rolled up and an envelope with some money in it. All Nancy could think about was how bad she needed money and there was enough cloth there to make some clothes for the children.

"I'll show you little miss Mary," she said out loud. "I'll take it all and never be the least bit sorry for it. I'll just consider it payment for lettin' you live here and eat my food and drank my water."

Her temper flared out of control as she jerked the bed cover off the bed and ripped it to pieces. Then she reached back in the trunk and pulled out Mary's white dress. It was her favorite and Nancy knew it. "Maybe one day, I'll make you a purty white dress like mine," Mary had told her one day.

Nancy had looked down at her faded gray dress that had been mended over and over again and felt like Mary was making fun of her. "I didn't want no damned old white dress," she thought, and she'd make sure Mary never wore hers again either. She began ripping the sleeves off the dress and, when she couldn't tear it no more, she went in the kitchen and found a knife and began cutting it. She was laughing madly, tears streaming down her cheeks with the excitement of what she was doing. She knew she wasn't quite herself at that moment, but it felt good. It felt damn good to destroy someone else for a change. To wreak havoc on someone else's life. She only wished she could be there tomorrow when Mary came home and seen how her life had been intruded on.

Finally, when there was nothing else left to destroy, Nancy stuffed the envelope of money in her pocket, gathered up the material and trudged back up the mountain. The cool night air felt good on her hot, sweaty skin. She smiled to herself, content to believe that what she had done was justified.

The next day Nancy was working in the garden when Mary returned home. Nancy looked up, only for a moment, and went back to hoeing the weeds, humming to herself. Then she heard the scream.

Mary came running out of the shack toward the garden. Nancy dropped the hoe and went to her.

"Why Mary, what in the world's a matter with you?" she asked calmly.

"Somebody's been in my house," she said, hanging on to Nancy's arm. "They cut up my dresses and the bed clothes and, and .."

Her voice trailed off, as she ran back into the house to check the trunk for the money. She sank to the floor, clutching her heart and sobbing. Nancy stood in the door watching her. She felt no remorse for what she had done. It actually made her feel good to see Mary wallowing in her pity.

"Lord a mercy, Mary," Nancy finally said, walking into the shack. "Who on earth would have done such a thang?"

"I don't know. I just don't know," Mary said. "I ain't done nothin' to nobody. Maybe it was just some stray soldiers passin' through or a gypsy. Maybe they was just hungry or somethin'."

But, when she glanced toward the shelf, she could see that no food was missing. "Did you see anybody pokin' around here last night, Nancy?"

"Never seen nothin'. Never heard nothin' either. But it looks to me like you done went and got somebody mad."

"But who?" she sobbed. "Who would be so mean as to steal my money and take the material I made that I was gonna sew my younguns clothes out of? Who would do such a thang?"

Nancy just shook her head, walked out of the house, and went back into the garden. First chance she got, she would dye the material, so nobody would suspect anything, and she would stash the money until her next letter came and people would just think that David sent it to her.

Mary was beside herself with grief and was even afraid to stay by herself. She wrote Elijah a letter, begging him to come home. But he couldn't get a furlough. She asked everybody in the valley if they knew who could have done this to her, and the same name kept coming up -- Nancy -- it's in her blood, they all said. But, Mary refused to believe them. She knew Nancy could be ornery, but she would never stoop to this level of cruelty.

Nancy heard the rumors spreading through the valley like wildfire. She knew they all thought it was her and she really didn't care. She was tired of trying to live up to Parker standards and Silver standards and all the standards that didn't mean nothing to her. Then she got a letter from David telling her to write to him about what had happened and who the neighbors thought had done it. Nancy knew that he knew good and well who the neighbors thought done it. She wrote him back and told him that he had hurt her feelings because he knew they all thought she had done it and it sounded to her like he believed them.

"I didn't do it," she swore to Aunt Sinda. "I ain't got no likin' for Mary, but I ain't gonna steal from her."

Sinda sure enough wished she could believe Nancy. But, she had seen the scorn in that woman's eyes every time Mary was mentioned.

"I shore do hope not Miss Nancy. Cause ifen you did and Mister David finds out, he's gonna be a heap mad at your white ass," she laughed.

"Oh, so you thank it's funny, do you?" Nancy glared at Sinda.

"Lordy be," Sinda answered, all laughing aside now. "What's got into ya girl? You is as mean as the old devil hisself anymore. Why that old heart a yours done be turnin' black. I be tellin' ya, Mister David be mighty sad right now ifen he wuz here. He been powerfully good to you and this be how you mess up his good name."

With that she got up and left, trudging down the mountainside mumbling to herself. Nancy knew Sinda was right, and she knew that somehow she had to convince all the neighbors that she was innocent. If she didn't, she would be alone again. But it didn't matter how many times she said "I didn't do it," they all still thought she did.

To make matters worse, David wanted her to get all the neighbors to sign a paper saying they didn't think she did it. That was the only way he would believe her. He wanted to believe her, but he knew she had a mean streak in her a mile long. He just didn't want his neighbors to think she had done it. How would he ever face them again if they believed his own wife had done such a thing?

Nancy had done a fine job convincing Mary that she had nothing to do with the robbery. She never even had to say it, she just went about getting new bed clothes for her, cooking for her and making sure one of the boys stayed with her at night. Even though all the neighbors thought that Nancy was guilty, as long as Mary didn't think so, they would just have to keep their thoughts to themselves. Out of respect for David, they all agreed to sign their names and send the paper to him saying that they didn't think she was guilty of the crime. This made David very happy and he was quick to tell Nancy how proud of her he was for all the work she had done around the farm and that he had believed her all along, he just needed to know that the neighbors believed her too.

David was very distraught to hear that Nancy Carrell was still living with Nancy. What in blue blazes was Nancy thinking now. He knew that he had told her to ask Nancy Carrell to stay with her to help with the children. But now, all the work was done for the winter and he wanted her gone. He had to make sure that Nancy and his children had enough to eat for the winter. He couldn't let other people live off them. He had tried to tell Nancy how to manage her money and her food, but sometimes he just didn't know about her. It seemed that she had just gone plumb mad since he left.

David had many friends in the settlement and they all wrote him letters. It just hurt his heart to no end when they would tell him things about his lovely little wife. If he was home she wouldn't be acting like this, even if it meant taking his hand to her. But he wasn't there and didn't know when he would get to be there. He was sick, had no food but dry crackers and a little beef, and was homesick. Then he would hear tell of Nancy doing such mean things as running a neighbor off their property just for killing a squirrel. She even shot and killed Matthew Smith's dog for getting one of her chickens. And her and Nancy Carrell talked bad about everyone in the valley. They even spread lies about the other women having affairs with men who had stayed behind while their husbands was at war. Now that was just wicked in David's opinion. It was hard enough for them to be out on the battlefields, leaving their womenfolk behind, without rumors of affairs and such going on. Sometimes he just didn't know if he wanted to go home or not. Seemed like Nancy was always into something. He would supply the neighbors with stamps when he could get them, then Nancy would charge them an extra penny for them. She was conniving, to say the least, but according to everybody in the valley, she was fairing better than the rest of them.

She had sold off most of their cattle so she wouldn't have to feed them through the winter. The best ones were killed for meat. She had made 17 gallons of molasses from their cane. She had managed to put up all the vegetables the cellar would hold and had all her corn gathered and cribbed. She had also saved enough money to buy leather to make them all shoes for the winter and she had sewed the boys new pants and the girls each a new dress.

Now if he could just get through to her how much he still loved her and how much his loins moaned for her attention, he would be satisfied, and perhaps that would put an end to all her shenanigans.

The end of the year was nearing and David feared he would be spending the winter in a camp near Fredericksburg.

December 17, 1862

...we was called to go to the battlefield Thursday the 11 day, but we was not called into an engagement till Saturday evening. The enemy had possession of the rail road that was there fortification. They had run our force out of thare. That day the 16 had to leave there and several other NC Regt. had to leave there too. But when the 54 and 57 went the yankeys had to leave there. We was marched up in front of them and thrown into line of battle in a half mile of their battery pouring the shell and grape on us all the time like a hale storm. We charged under the fire of the cannon firing four times a minute and the yankies pouring their miney balls round us like bees a swarming. We charged a distance

of about three quarters of a mile when we got in three hundred yards of the yankeys they took to their heels like scared turkeys. We run them to the top of a ridge and they had stoped about seventy five yards on the other side of the ridge. We run up to the top of the ridge and fired at them and then retreated back to the rail road and took our stand there to live or die before we would leave there. But they never came no nearer than the top of the hill just in sight of some of us. I tell you that balls sung over our heads like bees a swarming but I will have you to no that I made some sing around them too ...

... I can say to you that William Roberson got here one day before the battle commenced. I did not get to talk much with him. I can say to you that when he gets home if he ever does, he has some money for you that I sent by him, some fifteen or sixteen dollars, I don't recollect which. When you get it send me the amount. I got one of the pretiest little pocket books to send to you and put the money in it and gave it to William J. Thomas to give to William Roberson ...

Nancy set in the rocking chair in front of the fireplace, reading the latest letter from David to the children. They had come to expect to hear from their pa at least once a week. Bill and Charlie loved to hear the letters. They sat cross-legged on the floor, eyes wide with excitement, as they listened to how their very own pa was fighting the Yankees.

"Did he kill one Ma, did he kill one?" Bill asked, so excited that he quivered all over.

"Now, Bill, I told you, it ain't all about how many Yankees your pa kills," she would try to explain to him. "Ain't you more interested in knowin' that your pa's not sick and how much he misses us?"

"Well, I am," Bill said slowly. "But I'm more interested in the shootin' and the cannons!"

But, even in all their excitement, she knew the boys missed David as much as she did. She had hoped so badly that he would get to be home for Christmas. She had already made a pumpkin pie and a peach cobbler and she aimed to kill one of her finest hens to cook. She had knitted David new socks and had hoped that maybe he would bring something home for the children.

She supposed that it didn't matter much now. She had made Nancy Carrell go back home to her momma and Mary wasn't speaking to her again. Something about how she didn't want the neighbors mad at her because of things that Nancy was supposed to have said. That didn't matter either. Nancy didn't care if the whole damn valley hated her, but she was sure she would pay for it when David came home. At least, she still had Aunt Sinda, who had promised to come and eat Christmas dinner with them. Nancy had knitted her a new scarf to keep her neck warm. She would go into Burnsville at first light and see about getting the children a stick or two of candy, so they would have something Christmas morning. As for her, she would be content to wait on William Roberson to bring her David's gift. William was too old to go to war, so besides his bootlegging, he had pitched in for the cause, delivering mail to the rightful places. She could certainly use the money, but more importantly, it made her happy that he thought enough of her to send her a pocket book. She only wished that he would be the one bringing it and not a neighbor man.

December 25, 1862

Camp near Fredricksburg

Dear Wife, it is through the mercies of god that I am permitted this blessed Christmas evening to seat my self in order to answer your kind letter dated December 14. As for my health as the preasant it is not verry good. My bowells is hurting me again but I am better than I was some day or two ago. As for my health other wise, it is tolerable good, though I am verry weak at this time, hardly able to go about at all. I went through so much hardship while the battle was on hand. Thare was four or five nights that I never slept one hour each night. I received your kind letter the 23 day of December. I was glad to hear that you and the children are well. I hope that when these few lines come to hand that they will find you all well and doing well. I was glad to hear that you had your corn gathered and cribed. I think that it turned out very well. I think that you have a plenty to do you by being saving. I can inform you that the fight is over here and I have went through and is a live yet for which I think my god for if it had not been for him I don't think that any of us could went through what we did a no more of us to get killed than what did. I am sorry to have to inform you that Henry Carrell is dead. He was taken to Richmond to the hospital about the first of this month. Supposed to have the feaver. He died the 19.

I thought a while that I would try to get a furlough to come home though I don't think that it is worth while for I don't think that a man could get a furlough to go home if he was to try all his life. They won't grant any furloughs now at all. It may be that after while if we going to winter quarters that they may give furloughs. So I shall have to close for this time. Farewell

David Parker to Nancy Parker

CHAPTER EIGHT
1863

With January came the big snows. It snowed so deep that Nancy couldn't get down the mountain. The spring froze over as temperatures dropped below zero. All the wood that she and little Bill had managed to gather in for the winter was going fast. Somehow she had to get down to the barn to make sure the animals were taken care of. Nancy was frantically trying to figure out what to do when she remembered, a long time ago, when she was living on Ellijay, Jacob had made a pair of shoes that allowed him to walk in the snow without sinking or sliding. She was very little at the time, but remembered how fascinated she was when he carried her outside to show her how they worked.

She bundled Bill up and instructed him to go just beyond the house and cut her a few pieces of mountain laurel. She took some of the leather she had saved and cut it into small strips. She then bent the laurel and wove the leather through the middle of it. When she had finished, she tied them to her old high-top shoes and went outside. To her amazement, it worked. She made Bill a pair too, and that afternoon they made their way down the side of the mountain to the barn where she milked the cow while Bill put corn and hay out for the old mare and the few chickens that were left. Nancy was truly proud of herself and her boy as they carried the bucket of fresh milk up to the house trying hard not to spill one drop as they struggled in the deep snow.

They were both about froze to death by the time they reached the house. Their shoes were wet and water had seeped through the worn-out soles of Bills old shoes and the bottom of Nancy's wet skirt clung to her bare legs. Neither could feel their toes or fingers, and she feared frostbite may get a hold of Bill. But there was still work to do. She warmed herself by the fire for a few minutes then returned outside, leaving Bill by the fire to thaw out. She filled a large pan full of snow and carried it inside to melt for water. Then she made her way to the cellar David had dug out in the bank. Once inside, she looked at the shelves. With some dismay, she began counting how many jars of food she had left. David had not been able to send her much money for fear of having it stolen before it got to her. She only had enough coffee for a few more days. The sugar was completely gone, but that was ok, she still had plenty of syrup left for sweetner. Her cornmeal and flour barrels were almost depleted, though she knew if she could make it last until the weather broke she had enough money to buy a little more when she could get into Burnsville.

Nancy knew that it was going to be a tough winter without David. But she could either sit and worry about it or she could make sure that what she had lasted. Then a thought struck her. All the neighbors knew that she was pretty well set for the winter, what if they started stealing from her? She quickly dismissed that thought, took a jar of beans off the shelf and headed back to the house.

The children were warm for now but, come morning, she would have to figure out how to get in more wood for the fire.

When supper was over she sat down and began writing David a letter. She didn't want him to know her worries because the good Lord only knew what he was going through right now. She didn't even know when she would be able to get the letter out to him. That William Roberson feller was the mail carrier and there was no telling when he would be passing through again. All the same, she wrote David to tell him they were all doing well.

David was not fairing near as well. He had been deathly sick with his bowels since the battle at Fredericksburg. He just couldn't shake it, so his captain put him on cooking duties to relieve him from battle. He was getting plenty to eat, but the rest of his company was on little over half rations. They only got a pound of beef a day or a quarter pound of bacon, a pound of flour and a little sugar once in a while. Snow was 10 inches deep, so he wasn't getting any letters from Nancy, though he knew she was still writing them. He was so homesick, he could hardly stand it. He wanted to be on the mountain, taking care of Nancy and the children like a husband should. He hated this war, but could do nothing about it but wait for it to end.

Nancy hadn't seen any of her neighbors in near on a month. She and Bill had managed to get in a little more wood after the snow stopped. She was also rationing food, trying to make it last through the winter.

One cold, icy morning she was making biscuits with the last of her flour, when the door flew open and there stood Nancy Carrell. Her bonnet hung loosely around her neck and she had a shawl draped over her straight, brown hair. Her nose was red with cold and she was trembling all over.

"My Lord, what in blue blazes are you doin' out in this weather?" Nancy asked, ushering her over to the fireplace.

"It's Pa," she said, nearly out of breath. "He's been killed in the war." She collapsed to the floor, sobbing into her skirts.

"I know, I know," Nancy said, consoling her as best she knew how. "David wrote me such in December. I just couldn't git off the mountain to tell you."

"You knew?" Nancy Carrell looked at Nancy as if she wasn't hearing her right.

"Yea, I knew," Nancy said.

"All this time, you knew and didn't come tell us? Did you know before you made me leave?" she spat the words at Nancy in anger.

"Course not. How could you even thank such a thang," Nancy threw back at her.

Nancy Carrell softened a bit, remembering what she had really came for. "Me and Ma, we need food Nancy. Do you have anythang to spare?"

She was looking at Nancy with tears in her eyes, so pitiful that Nancy almost fell for it.

"That's what you came for? To beg for food?" Nancy tensed up, eyeing Nancy Carrell. She didn't look sick or starved.

"Well, the way I see it, I helped you put up all that food and stuff, so I should git a little of it. Don't you thank?"

Nancy stood up, planted her feet firmly, hands on hips and stared at Nancy Carrell. Now, Miss Carrell had seen Nancy all fired up before, but she was desperate, so she held her ground.

"Say somethin', anythang, but don't just stand there like an old bull a fixin' to charge!"

"Git out," Nancy said bluntly.

The children sat quietly, eyeing their mother. Little Myra began to whimper and Bill quickly picked her up and handed her to Charlie.

"Ma said for you to leave now," Bill said calmly to Nancy Carrell, stepping in front of his mother.

Nancy Carrell gathered her skirts, got to the door and turned around. "I just cain't believe you would turn your back on me Nancy

Parker, when I helped you out for months. You'll pay for this, you hear me. You'll wished you never came to this part of the damn country."

Nancy picked up the broom and headed toward her. "Git out, I tell ya. Git out and don't you come back, you hear me!" she shouted, as Nancy Carrell ran out the door into the cold.

Nancy was boiling mad. She was trying hard to take care of her family. How dare that woman come in here wanting food. She wasn't about to share anything with anybody. She had worked her fingers to the bone to make it through the winter, and nothing Nancy Carrell said to her would make her share her food with her. She should have thought about that when she was living off her land all these months instead of her own momma's. David was right to have her run Nancy Carrell off. He knew what would happen, and she knew she had to be more careful from now on or the whole dadjim neighborhood would be wanting what little she had left.

In a matter of days, everyone knew what Nancy had done and they sure enough held it against her. Nancy did feel bad that Nancy Carrell had lost her pa, but she couldn't help it that weather had not permitted her to go and tell them. It wasn't her fault that they hadn't put any food up or that Nancy Carrell hadn't stayed home to help her ma do a garden. It wasn't her fault that just about all the men in the valley was fighting this God forsaken war instead of being at home taking care of their families. Nancy Carrell was the least of her worries now. She had a family to take care of and she be damned if anyone was going to stand in her way.

By now, the entire settlement knew to stay clear of Nancy. She buried herself on the side of the mountain and took care of her children until the snow finally left and she could see bare ground. Then she mounted up the old mare and headed into Burnsville with a stack of letters in her hand. In them, she told David that all the neighbors had been good to her and the children. She didn't want him to know what was really going on here and she sure didn't want him to believe the things that others were bound to tell him sooner or later. He knew that her and Mary weren't getting along, only because Mary told Elijah these things in her letters. She, however, would not burden David with gossip. All he needed to know was that they were well and that they had enough food to do them through the winter.

Mary had took to staying with her ma over in McDowell County, so Nancy thought it fit to move back into the shack for the remainder of the winter. It was smaller, so they wouldn't need as much wood for heat, plus she wouldn't have to trudge up and down the mountain to get to the animals. David wasn't happy with her move, but Nancy just thought it would be best. Hell, he wasn't the one here, she thought, he had no idea how hard it was to trek up and down that mountain for everything. She and Bill had done it all winter and they were tired. She was just sorry she hadn't thought of it sooner. Her cellar was near cleaned out, her money was gone and she and Aunt Sinda had began to pull their vittles together to make their meals.

Finally in April, Mr. Roberson delivered a letter from David along with a leather pouch he had made with 50 dollars in it. He also sent the boys each a cap. They were so excited, they ran through the house pretending to shoot at each other until Nancy finally made them go outside.

David was still at a camp near Fredericksburg but felt sure that he would get to come home in the summer. Meanwhile, he instructed Nancy to go ahead and hire somebody to cut her some logs and to do the plowing. Nancy was relieved to know that she and Bill would have help, at least with those two chores. Charlie was old enough now that he could help plant and, perhaps, David would be home in time for harvest.

May 14, 1863
Camp near Fredericksburg, VA

   Dear wife it is through the mercies of God that I am permitted to seat my self in order to drop you a few lines which will inform you that I am well at this time. Hopeing that these few lines will come safe to hand and find you all well and doing well. I can say to you that I received your kind letter yesterday dated april the 30. It gave me great satisfaction to hear that you all was well and doing well. I can say to you that we have had a very hard fight here. It lasted seven days. The yanks made a general attact on us a distance of fifteen miles a long the line at several points at the same time. They had prepared 8 days rations every man and had them on there backs. Started to Richmond but we met them and told them that they could not go to Richmond at this time. But they said that they was going to go on to Richmond then. So we pitched in in order to show them that the road to Richmond was a hard road for yanks to travel and so they found it before we quiot them so they came to the conclusion that the road back a cross the Rapahanick was easier to travel than the road to Richmond. So they cross the river back with twenty five thousand less than they come across with. Our losses estimated at nine thousand killed and wounded and taken prisoner. Our colonel is dead. Died from wound. General Jackson is dead. Died from wounds. Wm J. Thomas had his left thumb shot off or he had to have it cut off a bout the middle of the long joint and S.M. Boon is missing supposed to be taken prisoner. We have seven missing supposed to be taken prisoner. We hunted the battle field all over for them but could not find them no whare so they must have been taken prisoner. Thare was ten of our company wounded. None killed dead on the field. Only one that was badly wounded. Some with there fingers shot off. Some shot through the legs. Some through the arms. B.B Young has resined and gone home and I hope that he will be conscriped the next day after he gets home and will have to carry a gun on his shoulder the balance of this war. We were in two hundred yards of our old camp ground whare we was in December at the time of the fight. We have been her 8 or 9 days. All is quit a long line at this time. The yankies keeps up a drumming and running of the cars day and night. What they are doing I can not tell. Though some thinks that they are falling back to wards Washington City. Though they may be moving up or down the river aiming to cross at some other point....

I hope it want be long till I will get to see all my old friends and neighbors assemble at Crabtree Meeting house one time more. Especially the members of Crabtree Church. I want to meat them all one time more. If that church has any praying people in it I want them to pray god to put a stop to this unholy war. I want them to pray for me while

they are praying for I tell you that this is a hard plase for a
man to live up to his duties as he is required of God for all
he can hear is cursing and stealing and card playing ...

By the first of May, Nancy had the fields plowed and the corn planted. Her shelves were empty now, but she knew that, before too much longer, they would have fresh vegetables. She was just glad to get through the winter. Her already skinny hips were a might smaller and she had a few more gray hairs, but other than that, she was doing alright. Sickness had evaded her and the children through the winter, and for that she was mighty thankful. She figured it was due to them staying indoors and not being around anyone. She spent those dark days of winter mostly learning the girls how to sew and quilt. At night she was so lonely she could hardly stand it. She would hold David's picture close to her heart and weep in silence. She just didn't know how much longer she could go on like this.

When the first signs of spring began to show, she hustled the children outdoors. It felt good to breathe the fresh air and it gave Nancy a brand new outlook on what was to come. She figured she had made it this far, she would keep going until the end. She was so revived with the coming of spring that she and the boys cleared the brush at the far end of the field and planted a large patch of wheat. Nancy didn't want to ever run out of flour again, so she figured if she could plant her own stand of wheat, she would have it ground and put it back for hard times.

Nancy Carrell stood in the shadows and watched Nancy and the boys work from sunup to sundown. She and her mother had survived the winter only because they still had a few good neighbors left who refused to watch them starve to death. When spring came on, these same neighbors helped them plant their own garden, so they would have some means of food come winter. She had made sure all of these neighbors knew that Nancy had turned her back on her.

"After all I done for her," she told Sarah Edge. "Why I kept them screamin' younguns and helped her with her washin' and her cookin', and what do I git? Not a damn thang, that's what."

"If I was you, I'd just let it go," Sarah told her. "You don't wanna go makin' Nancy mad or it ain't no tellin' what she'd be aimin' to do."

"I ain't a scared a her," Nancy snarled. "What kind a woman keeps it to herself when somebody's pa dies? And what kind a woman turns her back on a friend and neighbor when they're in need? A mean one I'll tell you. But that's alright. I can be just as mean, you wait and see."

Sarah just shook her head and let it go. Them two had been friends since Nancy came to Cane Branch, so she figured this little tiff they were having would pass.

But she was wrong.

Nancy's garden vegetables, corn and fruit trees did very well and she and Aunt Sinda had their hands full trying to keep up with it all. Nancy watched her wheat with great intent as it grew tall and swayed in the valley wind.

One evening, she had just put the children to bed and was rinsing off the last of the supper dishes when a distinct smell got her attention. Something was burning. She quickly dried her hands on her apron and ran outside. The red glow seemed to light up the meadow as Nancy's heart sank to her feet. She ran through the garden, into the corn field and stopped, sinking to the ground in despair, when she saw her wheat field going up in smoke. The snapping and popping seemed to wake the night as the flames reached towards the heavens. She could do nothing but watch it burn. She was so beside herself that she hadn't even noticed Bill and Charlie coming up behind her.

"I'll grab a bucket Ma, maybe we can save some of it!" Bill yelled to her, as he turned back toward the house.

"It's too late," she sobbed. "It's too late."

Charlie put his arm around Nancy's shoulders and stared into the fire. Bill returned with a bucket that he filled with water from the creek and put small embers out around the edge of the field so that it wouldn't spread to the corn. They sat there for hours, until the last spark died and only small circles of smoke swirled in the moonlight. Then they made their way back to the shack.

Nancy couldn't sleep at all. She just kept thinking about what could have started the fire. She wasn't surprised that no one came to help her, but she was surprised that no one even came to watch. That made her think that someone had burned her wheat on purpose. And there was only one person she could think of that would do such a thing. Nancy Carrell was as mad at her as anybody had ever been and she knew that Nancy Carrell had a mean streak herself. After all, she had loved the idea of Nancy breaking into Mary's house and she was the one always spreading all them lies about everybody.

When daylight came, Nancy marched right over the hill to Nancy Carrell's house. She didn't even bother to knock on the door, she just walked straight in to where Nancy Carrell was having her morning coffee with her mother.

"Why Nancy …," she started to speak.

Without a word, Nancy picked up her cup of coffee and threw it in Nancy Carrell's face. Miss Carrell screamed, knocking her chair over trying to get to the bucket of water. When she reached the bucket, Nancy grabbed the back of her head and plunged her face in the water. Nancy Carrell was trying to free herself, coming up long enough to gasp for air, then Nancy would cram her head back in the water.

"I'll teach you, you little hussy. You don't ever mess with me or my family again. Do you hear me?" Nancy screamed at her, finally turning her loose.

Nancy Carrell's mother was in the corner sobbing. Her daughter leaned limply against the table that the water bucket was sitting on. Her knees were shaking and she thought sure she was going to collapse.

"I'm sorry," she said, breathlessly. "I didn't mean no harm. I just wanted to teach you a lesson."

Nancy got right square in Nancy Carrell's face, so close that the water dripped from her hair onto Nancy's dress, and said rather too calmly, "I said, you don't ever mess with me or my family again. If I see you anywhere near my property, I'll shoot you deader than them there Yankee men my David is a fightin'. Do you hear me?"

Nancy Carrell sank to the floor like a beat up old hound dog. She couldn't find no voice in her to answer, so she just nodded her head.

With that, Nancy lifted her skirts and walked out the door she had came in only moments before. She trudged back across the hill, her head held high. No one, and she meant no one, would mess with her again. She could do without the wheat, she had made it fine last winter. What she couldn't miss out on was watching Nancy Carrell squirm. She laughed out loud, and even added a little skip to her walk, with that thought.

Nancy felt stronger than she ever had in her life. She was standing up for herself for a change, and taking care of her family as well as any man could and she was damn proud of it. David had even quit telling her how to manage the money or what to do on the farm. He knew she was doing well. He had got that much from the other men from Yancey and around that area. By now, she was quite the talk in these parts and she carried a reputation almost as bad as her momma's.

The one thing Nancy wanted to do was move back home on the mountain before winter set in. David was worried about the Yankees coming through there and destroying everything and maybe even killing them, so he felt she would be safer away from the road. He didn't think they would go up the side of a mountain for a woman and her children. Nancy figured he had enough to worry about, so the least she could do was put his mind to ease about their safety, and she wrote and told him such. She also told him that she had been offered 24 bushels of corn for the mule and that she had talked to a Mr. Bowdick about selling her some wheat. She didn't tell him about her own wheat field, she didn't want to bother him with such. He knew she had ran out of flour last winter, so she felt sure that he would allow her to purchase some extra this winter.

She and the boys, along with Aunt Sinda, moved their few belongings back up the mountain. Then she and Sinda began filling the cellar once again, while the boys set to mending the little shed that David built next to the house. He had intended it for wood and to hang meat to cure, which was all good. But seeing as how there was no meat to cure this year, Nancy figured she could use it for a barn. She could keep the old mare up here on the mountain and bring all the chickens up and the milk cow, and that way she wouldn't have to trek down the side of the mountain every day in winter.

David agreed for her to get rid of the mule for the extra corn and also for her to purchase the wheat. With the money David had earned from cooking and making jewelry and purses, Nancy was able to stock up a plenty on coffee and sugar. She had leather to make shoes for them all for the winter and she purchased cloth and yarn. Once again, she faired the best in the settlement. She just wouldn't be bothered by anyone, as she had proved over and over again that she was more than capable of taking care of herself.

Finally it was November and all the work was finished. Nancy and the children settled in for another long, cold winter alone. David was doing the same as he had written to her November 4, that they had put up winter quarters at a place called Culpepper Courthouse.

"Me and Lige and Squire and James Hensley and William J. Thomas and O.P. Carson is messing together. We have just finished us one of the best houses in camp. We have got it fired of so that we can live in it as comfortable as we could at home. We have got it bobbed tite and has got a good chimney to it that don't smoke one bit. I tell you that we at home while we stay here as for comfortableness. As for war news I have none to write you at this time. Nothing has transpired since I wrote last. All is quiet at this time and I hope that it will remain so the balance of this winter so that we can in joy ourselves in our new house..."

Nancy was glad that David finally seemed comfortable and would be warm for the winter. He had suffered so terribly the last winter. She only wished that he was being comfortable here at home. She missed him so terribly and hated the thought of spending another winter without him. She needed to feel his arms around her, keeping her warm in the night. But it wasn't meant to be.

She didn't hear from him again for a month. She worried tremendously, for snow had not yet set in, and there was no reason for her not to get his letters. She tried to hide her fears from the children, but they continually asked why their pa had not written. Nancy made every excuse she could think of until finally Mr. Robinson showed up with a letter in his hand.

Nancy was so excited, she could hardly contain herself as she gathered the children around her and began to read:

November 20, 1863
Point Lookout Maryland
Dear wife it is through the kind mercies of God that I am permitted to seat myself in order to drop you a few lines which will inform you that I am well. Hoping these few lines will reach your kind hands in time and find you and the children doing well. I have for the first time to inform you that I am a prisoner of war. I was captured on the Rapahannock River near Brandy Station on the eveing of the seventh and brought to this plase. I can say to you that thare is several of the Yancey boys her with me to. Lige, S. Hensley, J. Hensley, Wm. J. Thomas, J.M. Boon O.P.Carson George Roland. E. Boon was left in camp on guard. He was well. So I shall have to close farewell.

Nancy's heart fell to her feet. Charlie buried his face in his knees.

"Pa's a prisoner Ma?" Bill asked, as if he had not heard her correctly. "What's that mean, Ma?"

Nancy gathered her thoughts together for a second. She wanted to cry or run screaming through the woods, anything to keep from facing the truth. But she couldn't, for the sake of the children.

"It'll be alright," she finally said. "It just means that the Yankees have him in their camp. They won't kill him though, I'm about shore a that. I thank they'll keep him till they can exchange him for one of their own men back. That's what I thank will happen."

"Are you sure, Ma? Are you sure?" Bill questioned.

She sure enough hoped she was right. Snow may not have set in yet, but Nancy knew it was still going to be the hardest winter she had endured thus far.

CHAPTER NINE
1864

Nancy learned later that David and the other men had went to the river to fetch some water when the Yanks took them off guard and captured them. They had gotten too settled in, David told her. Too comfortable. They didn't even have their guns on them at the time and no one was standing guard over them. It was a stupid mistake, one that he would pay dearly for.

Nancy did not hear from David again until February. Christmas came and went. She tried to make it a special day for the children. She and Aunt Sinda cooked a good meal and she had a stick of candy for each child. But, truly, it was just another day. She wished so badly that David had been able to get her more money before he was taken prisoner. He had told her that he had a hundred dollars in his pocket, but was afraid to send it. She knew she would never see it, as the Yanks surely would have taken it from him when they captured him. She was trying hard to conserve the food that she had because things had gotten so high she was out of money to buy more. Beans were near five dollars a pound, taters were two dollars a pound and corn was almost 13 dollars a bushel. The price of meat was even more so than that.

Bill and Charlie had set traps in the woods and by the creek, hoping to catch anything that was eatable, and Nancy had took to going to the woods every morning with the gun hoping to kill a rabbit. Several times, she had came back with only a crow. But, once cleaned and cook, even the crows tasted pretty good. There just wasn't enough to go around.

Snow blanketed the fields of Cane Branch and temperatures dropped to below zero through January and February. Nancy had plenty of wood to keep them warm, it was the food she was worried about. She had to keep the milk cow fed so her milk didn't dry up, because she had to have milk for the children and also to make butter. Her chickens had to have corn so they would keep laying for her. She had put up syrup, but not as much as last year. She had extra flour and meal, dried beans and her canned goods. But with a family of six plus Aunt Sinda, she didn't know how long she could make it last.

Finally, the snow left and it began to warm up for a spell. It was the end of March so it wouldn't be long before Nancy could get the fields ready for planting, but their food was pretty near gone. She had rationed till she couldn't ration no more. The kids were hungry and she was hungry. She had killed all the chickens but two and they were looking mighty good. Her flour was almost gone, as was as all of her preserves. She still had a couple handfuls of dried beans and a few taters, but they were starving for meat.

One morning, she sent Bill and Charlie to check the traps, while she loaded the old gun and was headed for the woods once again to try and kill them some meat, when she spotted someone coming up the trail towards the house. She immediately raised the gun and took aim.

"It's just me, Silas McCurry. Don't shoot!" he called out to her, waving his arms in the air.

"What's your business here?" she asked, lowering the gun ever so slightly. "Ifen you come for food, I ain't got nary."

"I only come to let you know what I just heared," he said.

"And what might that be?" Nancy asked rather rudely. She wasn't in the mood to entertain company; she had work to do.

"Well, you heared a Kirk's Raiders, ain't you?" he asked. He sure wished she would put that gun down, it made him uncomfortable as he shuffled from one foot to the other.

"Maybe. Ain't he that damn Yankee that goes around shootin' women and children, and stealin' everythang he can get his hands on?" she asked.

"That's right," he answered. "Well, Colonel George Kirk, the leader of 'em, just attacked Morganton, and I hear his boys is headed in this direction. They say he's gonna make his way into Burnsville and raid the local warehouse and everybody else in the area. So, you need to hide everythang you got. I mean everythang, Nancy, or that group of Yankees will git it all."

"They'll not git nothin' I got," Nancy stated flatly. "I'll put a bullet twixt their eyes they come messin' around here."

"Nancy, please," Silas begged, "for once in your life, will you listen to somebody and quit actin' so tough and almighty? I'm a tellin' you that, if them boys come through here, you and the children better hide, for it ain't nothin' for them to shoot women and children a like. They ain't got no sympathy for nobody. Will you do that Nancy?"

Nancy thought for a minute. She would never put her children in danger. "I reckon I can," she finally said.

Silas tipped his hat, thanked her and headed back down the mountain to tell everybody else in the valley.

Nancy waited for the boys to come back, empty-handed again, and she told them they needed to take the cow and the old mare on up the mountain a ways.

"Far enough to be outa sight of the house, but not so far that we cain't git to 'em to feed," she instructed. "Then we're gonna cut some of this here mountain laurel and put in front of the cellar to hide it. Any belongin's we have that we don't want stoled, we need to put in the cellar. We may be hidin' out in there ourselves ifen them raiders come through here like old Silas says they're goin' to."

The boys set Nancy's plan in motion, while she and the girls gathered up pots, pans, silverware, everything they needed to live and put it all in the cellar. When the boys came back, she put them to cutting laurel while she headed down the mountain with her gun and a plan.

She went knocking on doors at all the houses where the womenfolk were fit, and asked them to meet her at the church that afternoon.

"Now, what are you up to Nancy Parker?" several of the women asked.

She just said, "You wanna live, don't you? We all about to starve to death and I got a plan."

They all knew too well how conniving Nancy was. But they also knew that if anybody could help them, it would be her. She wasn't afraid of anything.

When Nancy got to Nancy Carrell's house, she hesitated for a split second then walked up on the porch. Nancy Carrell slung the door open before she could knock.

"Don't you come over here startin' no trouble. I ain't done nothin' to you," she said to Nancy.

"I know you ain't done nothin'," Nancy told her. "I just need you to come with me and some of the other women to the church this evenin'. We're all starvin' and I got a plan to git what's rightfully ours in Burnsville, before them there raiders git to it."

"Have you done gone and lost your mind?" Nancy Carrell said, in surprise. "I ain't a goin' no place with you. Ma's sick and about dead and I don't want to git shot by no Yankees. Besides that, my uncle is part of the home guard in Burnsville and he'll never let us git near the warehouse where all that food is stored."

Nancy raised the old shotgun up on her shoulder and pointed it straight at Nancy Carrell. "Well, I'll tell you one thang, you'll either go with me or I'll shoot you myself."

Nancy Carrell began to back away, then she heard the hammer click on the old gun. She stopped, knowing that Nancy meant every word she said. Nancy Carrell started to cry.

"Please don't make me go Nancy," she pleaded. "I'll do anythang for you, if you just don't make me go."

"The way I see it," Nancy said, "it's all your fault that my younguns is hungry in the first place. So this is a fine time to pay back what you took from me. Now quit that damn whinin' and get on out here. We're meetin' the others at the church."

Nancy Carrell didn't want to move. She didn't want to go, but she knew she had no choice. That crazy woman was going to take her to the church with a gun pointed at her the whole way. What would people think?

"I said to come on now, we ain't got all day," Nancy said.

With that, Nancy Carrell grabbed her old shawl and followed Nancy down the path toward the church. She was just a mumbling to herself, sounded worse than Aunt Sinda.

"Quit that dadjim mumblin'," Nancy finally said. "If you got somethin' to say, say it loud enough so I can hear you."

"I was just sayin' that I thank you've gone plum mad Nancy Parker. Goin' without food has done made you crazier than you already was."

Nancy could have took offense to that, but instead she started laughing. "You may just be right Miss Carrell. You may just be right."

When they got to Sinda's place, Nancy stopped at the fence and called out to her.

Sinda came out on the old porch and when she saw Nancy with a gun and Nancy Carrell standing in front of her, she couldn't help but laugh.

"Good Lord child, whatta you gone and done now?" she said, laughing and slapping her knee. "I say, I reckon I done seen it all, I have."

"Aw, come on now Sinda," Nancy said grinning, "it ain't what you thank it is. I'm just takin' Miss Carrell here down to the church to meet with some other women folk in the valley and I want you to come, too."

The smile left Sinda's face and she frowned as she looked at Nancy. "What you up to now Miss Nancy? You gonna done git all us women in trouble one day."

"I just got a plan, that's all. Ain't nobody gonna git in no trouble if I can help it. Now you comin' or not?" Nancy asked, as she headed on down the road.

"Well, I's reckon I am. Cain't let you go by yourself. That Mr. David never would forgive me ifen I let you get killed. What's this plan you got anyway?" She asked, as she came up beside Nancy, already gasping for air. "And, you best be slowin' down, if you wants me taggin' a long. I's an old, fat lady. Cain't keep up with the likes a you skinny folks."

"Well, you ain't as fat as you used to be," Nancy chuckled. "And, that's one a the reasons I got this here plan. We all a starvin', so I figure it's time we done somethin' about it before them Yankees come in here and git what little food we do have left."

When they reached the church, several women had already gathered and when they seen Nancy coming with Nancy Carrell, they all began to snicker and whisper.

"Quit your laughin'," Nancy Carrell said angrily. "I tell you, I don't want to be here. But it seems Nancy has somethin' important to say and I thank we should hear her out, gun or no gun."

As Nancy talked, more women showed up, about 50 in all. Some old, some young, but all haggard and hungry. Seemed like since most the men were gone, the women just didn't much care about appearance anymore. Most of them wore dresses with rips and tears in them, holes in their shoes, hair greasy and fingernails dirty. They sure were a mess to look at and, for once in her life, Nancy knew she was doing the right thing.

"Now, listen up," she said loudly. A hush came over the church as Nancy explained to them how Silas had told her that Kirk's Raiders were heading into Burnsville to steal all the government food that was stored there for the soldiers. She knew the soldiers needed it, but they wouldn't get it if the raiders took it. "So as best I can figure, we need that food for ourselves. The home guard that watches over it is just a bunch a old men. I figure we can take them over, git all the food out we can, come back here and divide it up and be done with it, before Kirk's men even git here."

"Oh, dear Lord, I cain't do that," Nancy Carrell spoke up. "You cain't go pullin' no gun on my own uncle, Nancy, I won't let you."

"Well, then, I'll just have to let you pull it on him yourself, won't I?" Nancy said.

Nancy Carrell's eyes widened in fear. "You wouldn't do such a thang," she spat at Nancy.

Nancy raised the gun and pointed it at Nancy Carrell again, "Try me, why don't you Miss Carrell? Just you go on and try me, 'cause I've had just about all a you I aim to take."

Nancy Carrell clamped her mouth shut tight and hid behind Aunt Sinda.

The women began to talk amongst themselves. They all knew Nancy was right, but they had never done anything like that before. "What if we get shot?" one of them called out.

"Listen, we're all gonna die if we don't git some food in here," Nancy said. "I'd rather die knowin' I was tryin' to feed my family, as to let them damn Yankees have all the food. If they make it this far, we'll probably all die anyway. But at least we'll die with a full belly."

Who better to go stealing with than the meanest woman in the cove. Nobody else had it in them to do such a thing, and all the women knew that. If it were up to the rest of them, they would all starve to death.

So they agreed to help Nancy rob the county warehouse in exchange for their fair share of the food they took. There were about 10 of the women who had fairly good wagons, and they agreed to bring them to the church where they would all meet at first light the next morning.

Nancy didn't get much sleep that night. She was too busy planning the raid out in her head. Before daylight she was up putting something together for the children to eat while she was gone. She made a biscuit for each one of them and poured a small spoonful of syrup over each one. That was her last jar of syrup and it was more than half gone. Then, she cut two potatoes into chunks and placed them in the one pan they hadn't hid in the cellar and held them over the fire. When they were good and brown, she poured the last cup of beans, from the day before, over the taters. She spooned the taters and beans into the five plates with the biscuits. Then, she took her portion of beans and placed them on Rhetta's plate. Rhetta looked so frail these days, and when Nancy would ask her if she was sick she'd just say, "No Ma, I ain't sick. But I shore am hungry."

Several times Nancy had given her extra food, but she would take it off her plate and give it to Margaret Alice or Myra. She was only seven years old and it hurt Nancy's heart to know that she would let herself go hungry to feed her little sisters.

Nancy woke Bill and told him she'd be back directly. "Breakfast is on the table," she instructed him. "And you make shore that Rhetta eats everythang on her plate and don't let her give it to the others. By tonight, we should have plenty for everybody. But right now, I thank Rhetta needs it the worst or I'm scared she's gonna just lay down and die."

"Yes, Ma," Bill answered. "I'll make shore. I promise."

And Nancy knew he would.

She took her biscuit and closed the door behind her. She met all the women at the church. They may have all been scraggly, but they sure enough was excited. Nancy figured none of them had never even held a gun, let alone shot one, and she surely knew they hadn't none of them ever stolen anything in their life. She reminded them how important it was that, when they got to the warehouse, they all be quiet so the guards wouldn't hear them before they seen them.

Within an hour they were in Burnsville. Nancy instructed the women with the wagons to stay behind on the hill until they seen her signal to move in. Then she led the other women down to the warehouse where they were immediately confronted by an old man with a long gray beard. He was wearing overalls with holes in the knees and his bare feet were caked with mud. He looked like he hadn't eaten in days. His eyes were sunk back in his head and half his teeth were missing.

He didn't seem worried at all when he stepped in front of the door to stop the women. He had no idea what they were there for, so he just smiled a weak smile and asked them if they were lost.

That's when Nancy raised the gun and pointed it at him. "No, we ain't lost. Now drop that gun a yourn and don't move. You hear old man?"

The smile quickly left the old man's face. He dropped the gun and raised his hands in the air. Two other guards heard the commotion and came around the corner. They stopped dead in their tracks, when they seen all these starving women standing at the entrance.

"Drop your guns," Nancy shouted at them, "or I'll shoot him dead."

The men dropped their guns and Nancy instructed the women to tie them up with the leather straps Nancy had brought along.

"Is that you Nancy Carrell?" one of the guards asked. "What on earth are you doin' here?"

Before Nancy Carrell could answer, Nancy threw her a piece of leather. "You tie that one up," she said bluntly.

"But, Nancy," Nancy Carrell started to whine.

"I said do it," Nancy said angrily. She was determined to make Nancy Carrell forever regret burning her wheat fields.

Nancy Carrell took the leather. "I'm sorry Uncle Joseph. I have to," she said. Her hands were shaking almost uncontrollable as she tied her uncle's wrists behind his back.

"Well, don't just stand there," she yelled to the other women.

Three more guards came around the front of the building. The other women turned and saw them and began running toward them, shouting and flailing their arms. The fear had left them and they knew they had to help Nancy if this was going to work.

The home guards were so shocked at such a sight, they threw their guns down before the women even got to them.

Once they were all tied up, Nancy motioned for the others to bring in the wagons. She took the keys from the old guard's pocket and opened the warehouse. They filled the wagons with 60 bushels of wheat grain, about 100 pounds of fatback, several sacks of taters and dried beans. They worked quick with every ounce of energy they had in their weak bodies. Then the older ones climbed in the wagons where they could squeeze in, and headed back to Cane Branch, leaving the home guard tied up and wondering what exactly had just happened.

The women were back at the church before lunch dividing up their goods. Nancy took three bushels of the grain, about 10 pounds of the fatback, a whole sack of taters and a whole sack of dried beans, and put them in a pile 'till she could go get the boys to help her haul it all up the mountain.

"Sinda, you keep watch a my stuff 'till I get back," she said.

They were all watching Nancy.

"But, why do you git all that?" one of the women ask. "I thought we were splittin' it even."

"Well, I reckon you thought wrong, now didn't you?" Nancy said. "If it weren't for me, none of youns would have a thang and I got five other mouths to feed, plus Aunt Sinda here. So, don't be botherin' my stuff while I'm gone or I swear I'll shoot you."

None of them doubted her in the least bit. Honestly, they didn't think it would bother Nancy one bit to shoot any of them. And, they were right. They had all talked bad about her, even wrote David letters telling him things she had done. Hadn't none of them offered her any help when she needed it and now here she was helping them get food when they were starving. They should all be ashamed of themselves, and most were as they watched Nancy trudge up the road to get her boys.

"Wait a minute," Sarah Edge called out to Nancy. Sarah was Golden Edge's wife. She had brought one of the wagons that morning.

Nancy stopped and turned around.

"Put your stuff on my wagon Nancy and I'll take you to the foot of the mountain. That a way you won't have so far to carry it."

"Well I'll be," Sinda said. "They is some of you that has a heart."

Nancy never said a word as her and Sinda loaded the stuff in the wagon. When they got to the foot of the mountain Nancy turned to Sarah and said, "thank you Sarah, I'm much obliged."

"No, thank you, Nancy," Sarah smiled. "We might just be able to make it now."

For the first time in a long time, Nancy felt good. She couldn't wait to get home and fix a good meal for the children. They would eat until their bellies were full today. They could start rationing again tomorrow.

Kirk's Raiders showed up in Burnsville the next day. They marched in with about 75 men and took 100 rifles and what food was left in the warehouse. Then they moved on to Spruce Pine, never making their way into Cane Branch at all.

Nancy, and everyone else in the cove, was relieved to hear that news. Now they could unbury their treasures and go back to normal living, if you could call it that.

Here it was April already and Nancy hadn't heard a word from David since February, at which time he had been a prisoner of war for three months. He was doing well then and Nancy could only hope that he would be exchanged soon. She didn't have the money, nor could she promise anyone the money on David's return, to hire an abled body to plow her fields. Everyone knew that David had been taken prisoner, so no one in the cove would trust her to pay them. She and the boys would just have to do what they could to get ready for planting.

She had saved enough seed to plant and she had made sure the old mare had been fed good through the winter so she would be healthy enough to pull a plow. Once the ground thawed, she and the boys made haste with getting all they could in order. Bill was only 12 years old, but he was right handy with the plow and although Charlie was only 10, he could lay the rows out and help with the planting.

They worked from sunup 'till sundown with the help of Aunt Sinda and what little the girls could do. Nancy had to have at least part of the big cornfield planted to feed the few animals that were left. She would plant wheat back in what they had cleared the year before and she would plant plenty of cane, as that seemed to be what lasted the longest.

By the time May had ended, they were finishing the last of their planting in the vegetable garden. It had taken them almost two months to get it done, now all they had to do was pray to God that they would have a good crop.

Every morning Nancy would get up, fix a mighty slim breakfast and head to the fields. She was worn ragged and once again needing food. Meals of beans and biscuits just wasn't enough and, more often than not, at least one of the children were complaining with stomach pains. She was doing all she knew how to survive. She had only one chicken left and, before she let her kids suffer any longer, she had made plans to cook it for supper that evening.

She picked up the hoe and began to work. At least in the garden, she could be in her own little world where her thoughts didn't matter to nobody but herself. Sweat ran down her neck, wetting the front of her dress, but she ignored it as she continued to get the weeds out of her precious garden. She could see little spouts coming up through the dry earth and wished it would come a good rain. That's what they needed right now. A good slow, steady rain would make all her seed sprout and then she wouldn't have to worry so. She leaned against the hoe, picked up the tail of her dress and wiped the sweat off her neck. Then she made her way to the creek, where she took off her bonnet and dipped it into the cool water. She rubbed the wet bonnet on her neck before putting it back on her head, then cupped her hands and took a drink.

It felt so good, she didn't want to leave just yet, so she found a rock and sat down, putting her dirty bare feet into the cold water. She leaned back and closed her eyes, taking in the fresh air.

Plump. Something hit the water in front of her. She opened her eyes and looked around, but she didn't see anybody. It must have just been her imagination, she thought, and settled back on the rock.

Plump. There it was again and, this time, it was close enough to splash a few drops of water on her bare legs.

She jumped up, nearly falling into the creek, and there he was.

She thought she must be dreaming. But before she could gather her thoughts he had her wrapped in his arms. Together they sank to the ground, covering each other with kisses till their eyes met.

"My God, you are beautiful Nancy Parker," David said, taking her face in his hands and kissing her forehead.

"And danged if you ain't handsome, dirt and all," Nancy said, touching his face, then reaching to take his mangled hat off.

He was indeed a sight to see. His hair was matted and greasy, and he had a long beard. His clothes were ragged with holes torn in them. They were barely clinging to his body. His shirt had no buttons and he only had one suspender. His dirty toes were sticking out the ends of what was left of his shoes. But it didn't matter. Nancy still thought he was the best looking man she had ever seen.

Finally, they stood up and brushed their clothes off. That's when he really looked at his beloved Nancy. It almost brought him to tears to see her so frail. She looked like she had aged 10 years since he had been gone. Wrinkles creased her forehead and her eyes were black underneath. She had gray in her hair and dirt under her fingernails. She wore no shoes and her dress was almost threadbare. 'Damn this war," he thought as he pulled her close to him.

There was so many questions to ask. They wanted to know everything about each other. But the main question Nancy had was, "Are you home for good?"

With sad eyes he looked down at her and said, "No, I'm just on furlough. I have one month here, then I have to go back."

Nancy walked in silence. She was afraid to speak, afraid she would just break down and cry. She didn't want to ruin this moment with tears of sorrow, so she just squeezed David's slim waist with her arm as they continued towards the house.

Bill was making his way from the outhouse when he looked down the trail and saw his mother coming back with a strange man. Bill squinted his eyes, trying to make out who this could be. They was walking arm in arm as if … as if…

"Pa," he whispered, more to himself than anyone else. Then, he ran into the house screaming as loud as he could, "It's Pa, I tell you. Pa's home."

All five children came running down the trail toward David and Nancy. They were calling out for "Pa," screaming, giggling and crying all at the same time. David dropped his little pouch that held a cup, tin plate, two hard tact crackers and a piece of a comb. He fell to his knees as the children came to him in leaps and bounds. Nancy couldn't hold the tears back any longer as she watched the children so lovingly greet their father. She stood back and watched, tears running down her face. Little Myra clung to her mother's dress tail sobbing, and Nancy realized that Myra didn't know who her father was. She reached down and took Myra's little hand in hers and led her to David. The other children stepped back and watched as David lifted her onto one knee.

"It's me, Myra," he said, gently stroking her dark curls. 'I'm your pa."

Little Myra reached up and touched his beard. Then, she poked his cheek with her finger, and finally, she threw her little arms around his neck and he squeezed her to him. Tears welled up in his eyes for a moment, then the other kids wrapped around him and it was the happiest time of his life.

After a while everyone settled down and they made their way into the house. David was tired and hungry, but first things first.

"Go and fetch me the tub," he told Bill. "First thang I want is a good bath and a shave."

While Bill went to get the tub, Nancy and the girls headed for the spring, with every bucket and pot they could find, to fill the tub with water.

While David bathed, Nancy went out and killed the last old hen. "It's a day for celebratin'," she thought as she plucked the feathers, while Bill and Charlie commenced to telling David about how their ma had got all the women in the cove to help her go get food. David couldn't help but laugh when he thought about how they all must have looked going in on the home guard.

They were all laughing and splashing water on the floor out of the tub when the front door flew open and there stood Aunt Sinda with a rolling pin raised in the air, ready to strike. "Who are you and what you doin' here?" she yelled out.

Before David even thought, he stood straight up out of the tub. Buck naked as he was, he didn't know whether to go for his gun or run. Then he realized who it was.

"Sinda, it's me David. What in tar nation are you doin', comin' in here like this!" he yelled at her.

Sinda stopped dead in her tracks. She looked David from his head to his ... well as far down as she could see, and quickly covered her eyes and started laughing.

"My Lord Jesus in heaven, if it ain't Mister David done come home," she said. "I shore is sorry for bustin' in here this away, but I heared all that screamin' and carryin' on and I thanks to myself, some of them there Yankee men done come up this here mountain and be hurtin' my Nancy and the children."

"Well, you can calm down now," David said as he lowered himself back into the tub. "And you can open your eyes too," he chuckled.

Aunt Sinda just couldn't contain herself. She ran to the side of the tub and threw her big arms around David's neck, nearly choking him to death.

"I's just so glad to sees you," she said, picking up her skirt tail to wipe the tears from her eyes.

Nancy came in the back door. "We're gonna feast today Aunt Sinda," she said, holding up the dead chicken.

"Lordy day child, I reckon it is a day to feast. I's got me a couple chickens left. I'll go fetch another un and sees what I got yet in my cellar and I'll be back," she said, as she headed out the door with a new dance in her step.

"Oh happy day, oh happy day," she sang.

David finished his bath and his shave. He spent time with all the children, sitting first one and then the other on his lap in the old rocking chair. The boys were eager to hear about the war, but David told them they would have to wait until the girls were gone to bed. He didn't want his little ladies to hear any of the gruesome details of the war. He had seen many things while he was gone, half of which he would never speak of to anyone.

That evening they sat down to a meal fit for a king. They fed on chicken and dumplings, corn pone and pinto beans. Then they opened Sinda's last jar of peaches for dessert. They didn't have heaping plates full, but they had plenty to give them a good night's sleep.

For the next month, David spent most of his time downing trees, so there would be plenty of wood in the shed. He didn't have any money on him at all, the Yanks had took it all when they captured him, so he had no way of buying anything for his family. He could, however, make sure that while he was home, he got things ready for the winter. He couldn't do much in the fields as they were already planted, but he mended the barn and the house. He went hunting with the boys and showed them how to lay low for as long as it took, to wait for a rabbit or squirrel. One day he even pulled a big rattler out of some rocks and showed them how to skin it and eat it. Anything they could do to survive, he told them. "I had to eat rats while I was in that prison. They really weren't that bad once you got used to them."

"Really, Pa?" Charlie asked, wrinkling his nose up at the thought.

"I could eat a rat," Bill said. "When I go to bed at night and my belly starts hurtin' 'cause it's hungry, you dadjim right I could eat a rat."

"Well let's hope you never have to," David said, patting him on the back.

He hoped he never had to again either, but he couldn't be sure of that. He knew he had to go back to the war, but he sure enough prayed, every night, that it would end before then. Night after night he lay in bed holding Nancy close to him. He just couldn't face having to let her go again. He knew Nancy had changed since he left. It was like she had put up a wall around her so that no one or nothing could touch her. He no longer had the timid, quiet little woman that he had married and that's when he realized how tough this war had been on those left at home. Sure, he had struggled to stay alive on the frontlines. He had seen his buddies blown into pieces next to him. He had seen the creeks run red with blood. He had been sick and lonely and homesick. But what about his wife and children?

Every night he would watch his children sleep and wonder what was going through their little minds. He knew they couldn't possibly understand why he had left. All they knew was that he was back and, because of that, they thought things should be better. But he couldn't make them better. He knew they too had struggled to stay alive. They too had seen sickness among them, lost neighbors and friends, and been lonely without him.

Each morning only brought him closer to the day he had to leave. He tried not to think about it, and so did Nancy. She busied herself with the children and her chores. She worried about every meal she had to fix, wondering how much longer they could hold out. At least she was starting to get a few little vegetables here and there. She never before realized just how good a juicy tomato or green cucumber tasted. But, still she rationed. She mended David's clothes as best she could, for without money she had no way of getting cloth for new ones. She took what little bit of leather she had left and wrapped his shoes to cover the holes in the toes and put some padding on the bottoms.

Finally the rains came. But, along with the rains, came the day that David had to leave. It was heartbreaking for the entire family. Even Bill couldn't hold back the tears when his pa shook his hand, then hugged him to him. He was so proud of Bill and Charlie. They were so young, but they had done good for the family.

All the children cried. Nancy cried. David cried. Aunt Sinda cried. Then he set them all down and told them what he expected of them. The boys, he said, was to do just what they had been doing all along. It was up to them to keep wood in the house, go hunting for meat, help harvest the fields and anything else Nancy needed of them. The girls were to keep the house clean, mend and wash the clothes, help put up all the harvest and anything else Nancy needed of them.

He knew Aunt Sinda had been a help to Nancy from the beginning. To her, he just asked to remain a friend to Nancy. He commended each one on the way they had helped each other through these rough days and wished it to continue.

Then he had to say goodbye. Nancy walked down the trail with him to the bottom of the mountain. They held each other long and hard. She felt as though her very heart would break in two.

Once again they promised to write each other weekly, though they knew their letters didn't always reach each other. He promised to send money as soon as he could.

Their lips touched and he was gone.

Nancy watched 'till he was out of sight. Then she watched some more as if expecting him to turn around and come back. But he didn't. He was gone and she was alone again.

She picked up her skirts and trekked back up the side of the mountain. An eerie hush had come over the valley, and Nancy wished that things could be like they were when she and David first came here. She turned and looked at the rolling fields that at one time had been full of lush green corn. Now most of it was grown over with weeds. There were no cattle in the fields, no pigs to slop or chickens to feed. She wondered if it would ever be the same again, knowing in her heart that it probably wouldn't.

David walked through Burnsville and, as he passed the warehouse Nancy had robbed, he chuckled to himself. He just couldn't believe that she had done that. Then again, he could. She had always had a bit of a mean streak in her. He wished so badly that she would have had her likeness taken for him so that he could carry it in his pocket. For the life of him, he couldn't figure her out sometimes. She didn't want no picture taken of her because, she said, it didn't matter to anybody what she looked like. He was sure it had something to do with her mother, but he wasn't about to tell her that. He could understand why she didn't want anybody knowing who she was now or 100 years from now. But he sure would have liked a picture of her just for himself.

It took David a couple of days to get to the head of the road, where he could take the train to Salisbury. He rested in the boxcar while he chewed on a cold biscuit. By 8 o'clock, he and a few other soldiers traveling the same train, were in Salisbury, where they spent the night. At 10 o'clock the next morning, they took the cars to Raleigh. It took them until 10 o'clock that same evening to reach

Raleigh, where they spent the night. From there, they traveled to Weldon, then, to Petersburg, Va. They couldn't take the cars all the way into Petersburg because of the Yankees shelling them, so they had to walk the last four miles to report in. They were then put up at the home of a North Carolina soldier, where David finally got a letter out to Nancy telling her about his trip. He figured eventually they would go on to Winchester, Va., but he wasn't sure when.

That letter was dated July 26, 1864. The next letter he wrote was dated August 4, 1864:

Dear wife and children

It is with pleasure that I seat my self in order to drop you a few lines which will inform you when at hand that I am well. Hopeing that these few lines will reach your kind hand in due time and find you and the children all well and doing well. I can say to you that I have got to my regiment. I left Richmond the 27 day of July, took the cars for Stanton, 136 miles. We then had to walk 104 miles to Bunker Hill, 18 miles below Winchester. We got to our command last evening. We then received orders to march this morning. By day light we marched to this plase 8 miles from the Potomac River. We stopped here to cook rations. I can not say whare we will go from here. We may cross the Potomac in to Maryland.

I am sorry to have to inform you that when I got to the regiment William Thomas was not thare. He got killed or wounded and taken prisoner in a fight that our division had with the Yankees below Winchester 3 miles on the 20 of July.

The Yankees out numbered our men and whipt them and held the battle field. Killed several and wounded several. It is the opinion of the rest of the boys that he was killed. He never has been heard of since the rest of the Yancey boys is here and all well.

Our regt. Is very small at this time numbering about 120 here. Our company 25 here. I can inform you that we gained a great victory at Petersburg last Saturday. I can not give you the casualitees at this time as I have not time to write a full letter. I will have to close by saying I remain your true husband until death.

Nancy received both letters at the same time. She was so relieved to hear that David had gotten back to his regiment, but she was saddened at the mention of William Thomas. She was always saddened at the loss of anyone from Cane Branch. They had been her neighbors and her friends until this godforsaken war started. Now they were all dying one at a time, until there would be nobody left to keep the valley alive but the women, and they were doing the best they could.

Nancy, Sinda and the children all worked hard in the August heat. They put up everything they could get their hands on for the winter. There was still no money. They were all barefoot and their clothes threadbare, but still they worked. And, when evening fell each day, they would jump in the creek to cool off and bathe the dirt off them.

When David was home, he had ask Kitty Black if she would help teach Bill and Charlie to read and write. Kitty was well-learned and had helped Bill a little before the war started. Nancy had tried to keep up with his lessons, but with all she had on her, it was almost impossible until the winter months. Nancy hadn't had much schooling herself, but she could read enough to keep up with David's letters and she could write about as good as he could, only most people didn't think so. She wasn't one to let everybody know her business and she figured whether she could read and write or not shouldn't matter to anybody else.

But if David wanted Miss Kitty to teach the boys, then she would make sure they learned. It would give them something to do when cold weather set in and David promised to bring them both a knife when he returned, if they would keep up with their lessons. He also promised the girls some rings as long as they were good and helped their mother.

Nancy's corn and cane was doing well and she had plenty of turnips and cabbage. She had her wheat sowed, but it wasn't coming along as well as she had hoped.

Sinda knew Nancy was worried about the winter and she figured there might be something she could do about it. One morning, bright and early, Sinda put on the best dress and apron she had and walked into Burnsville to the Nu Wray Inn. She had seen the inn many times, but never had the nerve to actually go in the spacious white boarded building. Today was different. Somewhere along the way, Sinda had picked up some of Nancy's spunk and she walked into the inn like she owned the place.

She rang the little bell at the front desk and waited. Directly, a short, little white woman came around the corner.

"What can I do for you?" she asked, looking Sinda from her head to her toes. She wasn't used to seeing no black women at the inn unless they worked there. Everyone who came to the inn to stay were prominent folks in suits and ruffles.

"I's lookin' fer work," Sinda said, holding her chin high.

133

"I's a free person of color," she said, laying the papers on the desk for the woman to see. "And I's one a tha best cooks in this here country."

"What makes you thank I need a cook?" the woman asked.

"I don't know that for shore, ma'am. I just knows I need work and I like the looks a this here place."

The little woman laughed. There was something she liked about Sinda. "Well surely you must know that we ain't gettin' much business these days 'cause a that cussed war. Been doin' all the work around here myself, since the mister been deliverin' mail back and forth to the soldiers. Says that's the least he can do, since he's too old to fight. Anyway, I reckon I could use the help and the company. You got a place to live?"

"I have me a cabin over yonder on Cane Branch," Sinda answered.

"Well, that's too far for you to walk every day," the little woman said. "How about you just stay right here with me. You can help me with the cleanin' and the cookin', and I can give you a room and feed you. You can have one day a week off. I'll try to pay a little something along. Cain't promise you that every week though, you know times is mighty hard. But I figure after this here war is over we'll have plenty a folks comin' to visit, then I can pay you what you're worth."

Sinda thought for a minute, then told the woman she could start in two days. She had to have time to get things in order at home. The little woman agreed and Sinda left the inn feeling sprite indeed. This was one winter she wouldn't have to worry about being cold or hungry. And, if things went as planned, she would be able to carry Nancy and them younguns some food occasionally, even if it was just leftovers from the guests.

She went straight to Nancy and told her that she had taken a job at the inn. Nancy was excited for Sinda, but sad that she wouldn't be around all the time. But, Sinda promised her that she would come on her day off and check on them.

"Ifen you need anythang atall, you knows where to find me," she told Nancy.

Then she left the mountain and went to her cabin. She gathered up what little food she had left to give to Nancy. She didn't have any animals and she had very little clothing. But she was happy. She knew this was the right thing for her to do and she was mighty proud of herself for even thinking of it.

David finally had some money, but he was afraid to send any to Nancy by way of a letter. He wrote her and told her that he drew 53 dollars in wages, but they had deducted 31 dollars from that because he was late getting back to the regiment from his furlough. He knew she needed money worse than he did and he promised her to get it there somehow.

Day in and day out, she waited for someone to show up with the money. She needed it to buy cloth to make clothes and leather to make shoes for the winter. She needed to stock up on flour, coffee and meal. But it didn't come.

The next time she heard from David he was in the hospital in Lynchburg, Va. He had taken a bullet in the arm at Winchester. Several had been wounded that day in September and some had been killed or taken prisoner. Nancy was just thankful that David had only been injured, though she knew that was hard on him too. He told her she could write him back if she wanted, but he thought he might be home before the letter got to him. That gave her some hope as the days pressed on.

Late one evening about the first week of October, the wind was howling through the trees, the boys were trying to read by candlelight and the girls were asleep when Nancy heard someone step up on the porch. She grabbed the old shotgun leaned against the fireplace, and instructed the boys to be quiet. She was almost to the door when it flew open, as if from a hard gust of wind, and there stood her David.

She ran to his side and helped him into the house. His arm was in a sling and he looked almost as haggard as the last time he had came home. The boys gathered around him, wanting to know how he got shot. He laughed and patted them on the head.

"How 'bout we talk about it tomorrow?" he told them. He sure was proud to see them reading. He would give them their knives tomorrow, but right now he was cold, hungry and tired.

While Nancy set to making him something to eat, she told him about Aunt Sinda taking a job at the inn. He was glad to hear that she was doing well, but he was sorry that Nancy would be alone through the winter.

That night, he held her tight against him. It had only been a couple months since he laid with her, but it felt more like a year. He missed her so deeply and wanted her so badly that it didn't take him long to raise her gown and make her his own again.

Afterwards, Nancy lay cuddled against his chest and listened to him breath. This is what she wanted for the rest of her life. David was her strength, her everything. She fell asleep wondering how long she would get to keep him this time.

Morning brought much sunshine to the Cain Branch mountain cabin. The girls never expected to wake up and see their pa and the boys couldn't wait to hear how he had gotten wounded. Nancy had a much better outlook on things. She knew that, for at least the first part of cold weather, she would have David there to help her. His arm was in bad shape, so he couldn't do a lot, but just being there was enough for Nancy. He could keep them safe, keep the fire going, help occupy the children and snuggle with her at night.

Together they figured out food rations for the family so they would have enough to last them until late spring. That's if all went well. In these mountains, no one could bank on anything through the winter and them damn Yankees could come tearing through the area at anytime and steal everything they had. That's why David convinced Nancy to put the laurel bushes back over the cellar door. That's where he wanted all the food kept.

He went hunting and trapping with the boys, though just about all the wildlife had been killed out. Meat was the one thing he missed, for his regiment had always had meat, even though in small portions at times. He had brought money home with him this time and wondered if there was any pork to be had anywhere in the area.

They left the cabin early the next morning and set out on foot to Burnsville. This was quite a treat for the children because Nancy never took them with her into town. The only place they had been in months was to church when Sinda would take them and to her house. The rest of the time they spent in the cabin, playing in the woods or running through the fields.

They chattered happily as they skipped along beside David and Nancy. When they reached Burnsville, they made their way to the inn to see Sinda.

"Well, I declare, if it ain't Mister David," Sinda yelled from the porch, leaning her broom against the rail and coming out to greet them.

"I'm shore glad to see you doin' well, Aunt Sinda," David said. He had never seen Sinda look so good. She had on a long, black dress with a clean white apron over it. Her hair was pulled up in a bun with a little white bonnet covering it. She was spic and span clean and smiling from ear to ear.

"Yes sir, this be one winter old Aunt Sinda won't be starvin' or freezin' to death," she grinned. "Now, tell me what happened to that there arm a yourn."

"Well, you know it's just part of war, Sinda. It's just part of war," his voice faded off as he went into deep thought about his buddies still out there fighting.

"Well, let's just not talk about it," Sinda said, taking his good arm and leading them into the inn.

She introduced them to Miss Lucy and gave them each a small glass of water. David asked if either of them knew where he could buy a hog or some pork meat. Lucy told him to check at old Royal's store down the road a piece.

"There ain't much comin' into these parts nowadays, but you might git lucky," she said. "Old man Royal, he tries to keep stuff hid for the locals."

They chatted for a short spell, then David and his family walked down the road to the store. Sure enough, Royal had a little pork put aside, so David bought several pounds of fatback, a sack of flour and treated each child to a stick of candy. There was no leather to be found, so he bought the oldest boy and girl a new pair of shoes. He would pass their old ones down and take the youngest ones shoes to patch the other ones. He and Nancy would just have to make do with what they had. Nancy picked out a spool of cloth to make the boys a pair of britches each. She had saved a couple of flour sacks to make dresses for the girls. She would take their old clothes and cut them up for quilt tops.

Before heading back home, they stopped back at the inn for a bowl of Sinda's vegetable soup, seasoned with beef meat, and a biscuit.

By the time they reached the mountain cabin, they were all worn out. It had been a good day for them, one that Nancy would not soon forget. She knew that as time went on, David would have to leave again.

That day came on a very cold, blustery morning the first week of December. His time was up and he knew if he didn't get back they would dock his wages again. He reminded Nancy to keep doing the rations they had planned out for the winter and she would be fine. He could hardly contain himself as he hugged each of the children.

"Please stay Pa," Margaret Alice pleaded with him.

"I wish I could, more than anythang on this earth," he said, kissing her forehead. "But it is my duty to go. Someday you'll understand."

They all gathered on the porch and watched as Nancy and David walked hand in hand down the trail towards the road. Little Myra laid her head on Bill's shoulder and cried, wondering if she would ever see her pa again. She was far too little to understand why he was leaving them again, but she would forever carry that image in her mind.

David hugged Nancy close to him. He sucked in the smell of her hair against his cheek and the feel of her small frame against him. If only he could keep this moment in time forever. He didn't want to let her go, he just wasn't ready. Tears flowed silently down Nancy's cheeks. She was so afraid to let go of him, afraid it would be the last time she would feel his arms around her.

"I will forever love you Nancy Parker," David whispered in her ear.

"And I will forever love you," Nancy said, lifting her lips to meet his.

They stood in the snow, wrapped in the warmth of each other's love, swaying to the sound of the wind whispering through the pines, till finally, they had to let go.

Nancy watched as David walked away. He wanted to turn around and look at her one last time, but he was afraid if he did, he would run back to her and never leave. His heart told him to do just that, but his pride and honor told him to move forward, he had a job to finish. So he walked on, staring into the snow ahead of him, praying to God to take care of his family while he was gone. Praying to God that this war would be over soon and he could come back home to them. Praying to God for His almighty protection when he once again faced his enemies.

Nancy watched David disappear into the shadows. Tears continued streaming down her face as she laid her hand on her belly. She could almost feel the baby growing inside her. She knew she probably should have told David, but she just couldn't, not now. She felt no joy in her heart as she turned and walked back toward the cabin. The only hope in her despair was that he would come back to her. Come back to her and the children for good.

CHAPTER TEN
1865

Life went on as it had for the last two winters. Things were getting worse as the war went on. There was no trade at all going on between the North and the South, so there was no more goods to be had anywhere. If folks didn't have coffee, sugar and flour stored up, they did without. When what they had stored up was gone, they did without. Nancy had rationed her food like she and David had planned, but they were still hungry. But at least folks on Cane Branch had not taken to stealing from each other like they had in other parts of the country. For that, Nancy was thankful.

The boys busied themselves with reading, writing, hunting and trapping, while the girls worked on a quilt made from scraps of their old clothes. They had put the word out to all the neighbors that if anyone needed any mending or sewing done, they would be glad to do it at a fair price. But no one had any money, so even the most well-off folks were doing their own mending and sewing.

Nancy was beginning to show a little and she worried endlessly about the following months. How on earth would she be able to work the fields come spring? She was as tough as an old hickory nut, but if she wanted to birth a healthy baby, she would have to take care of herself. There was barely enough for her kids to eat, she had no idea where the nourishment she needed would come from.

She had written to David, but couldn't find it in herself to tell him that she was pregnant, though she knew he would be excited about it. She didn't want to put that worry on him, so she kept it to herself until one Saturday morning when Aunt Sinda came to visit.

"Git on in here," Nancy said, opening the door. "You'll catch your death out there."

The wind slammed the door shut and Sinda rushed over to the fireplace. Her fingers were blood red from the cold and snow clung to the sprigs of hair sticking out from under her bonnet.

"What on earth brings you way out here in weather like this?" Nancy asked with her hands on her hips.

"Now, don't go gettin' all high and mighty on old Sinda," she said, pausing to catch her breath. "I jest thought you all might need some food, so I been savin' every little pinch I could git my hands on at the inn, and I just figured now was as good a time as any to bring it to you."

She handed Nancy the large basket she was carrying. Nancy set it on the table and took the cloth off the top. The children gathered around, excited to see what Sinda had brought. Lo and behold, there was biscuits and fried bacon. There was apples, coffee grounds, little glass bowls filled with peas, rice, potatoes, soup with chunks of beef in it and even a half a block of butter.

"Can we eat it Ma, can we eat it?" Margaret Alice asked, reaching for a half-eaten apple.

"Shore you can," Sinda answered before Nancy had a chance. "That's why I's brung it to you, so yous could eat till yous couldn't eat no more."

Sinda laughed and slapped her knees. It made her very soul sing to be able to bring this family something good to eat. Then she took a good hard look at Nancy. There was something different about her.

Sinda's smile faded and concern took its place. "Nancy, you feelin' alright child?"

142

"Never felt better in my life," Nancy lied. But Sinda saw right through it.

"Come ear. Sit down and tell Sinda all about it."

"There ain't really nothin' to tell," Nancy said, pulling a chair up to the fire.

Sinda looked into Nancy's eyes and she knew. "You with child, ain't you?" she asked.

"How'd you know that?"

"Well, for one thang, you a little bit bigger and for another thang, I sees it in your eyes. Cain't git nothin' past this wise old black woman." She paused for a second. "Now whatcha gonna do with another baby, Nancy? How you gonna take care of anotherun?"

"I don't rightly know Sinda, but I reckon I'll figure it out."

"Do Mister David know?"

"No, and don't you be tellin' him either! You hear me?"

"I ain't sayin' a word," Sinda said. "And, yous know I be right here to help you when the time comes, don't you?"

Nancy did know. She knew Sinda had always been there for her, and she would be there this time too.

Sinda left in time to get back to Burnsville before dark. She took the empty basket back with her, hoping to fill it again soon for Nancy and the children.

Nancy took some of the coffee grounds, poured hot water over them and sat down in front of the fire. She took David's last letter out of her apron pocket and read:

January 2, 1865

...Times is getting very hard here. Rations is getting very scares. I think they have been giving us crackers for the

last week. They say that is no flour in Petersburg to get. Though at this time we are getting very fair rations. We get coffee enough for one meal per day and I am more ready enough for twice a day and we get shugar and rice and one third of a pound of bacon pork or pickeled beef or one pound of flour or one pound of crackers per day. We could do very well if we had bread enough. We could make out for other things. I think that this war is bound to come to a close some time this winter or spring. However, I hope it will so that I can get home one time more to stay at home and help you raise my children. For it looks like if this war goes on much longer that you and them boath will go necked and perish too. So will close by saying I remain your true husband until death.

David Parker

She read it again and again. Her heart was pounding as she remembered how his arms felt around her, and she yearned to feel that once more. Each time he came home and left, it was a little harder to let him go. How long she could go on like this, she did not know. But she knew if things were getting harder where David was, then things would be even more so here in the South. So she set her mind to thinking about how she was going to make it through till spring.

The next morning, she sent the older children out to all the neighbors asking if they needed any work done in exchange for food. The boys were old enough to split wood or carry water, and the girls could help cook or sew. But nobody needed them, so they all went home that evening, tired and hungry. That didn't stop Nancy. Every

144

day, when weather permitted, she sent the children out. She knew that eventually, somebody would need something. But day in and day out, the children returned home empty-handed.

Finally when March rolled around and the ground thawed a little, the boys began working to clear gardens for the neighbors. They would work for food usually, but sometimes folks would pay them with a piece of old clothing or a pair of worn out shoes, just whatever they could find that was of no use to them. But Nancy put it all to use. If the clothing couldn't be mended for one of them to wear, then it was cut up for quilting. The same with the shoes. Nancy saved every piece of leather she could get her hands on to mend the children's shoes so they would last until warm weather. When the children didn't have work for other people she put them to work in her own fields. She helped all she could and so did Sinda when she came to visit, and she always brought them a basket of leftovers from the inn.

David had written to Nancy throughout the winter months, and she always answered him back, though he didn't always get the letters. As far as she could tell, he was a sharpshooter guard at night in the ditches outside of Petersburg, Va.

March 19, 1865

... We are one mile from Petersburg in the ditches. Our breastworks and the Yanks in front of us is not more than three hundred yards apart. In front of the sixth regt. And the right of us some hundred and fifty yards apart. A man dare not raise his head above the breastworks if he does he will be shot at shore. We have port holes to look through on last Thursday the yanks put up white flag on their works and got

145

up on them works and shook their newspapers. Our men then put up white flag on our works and wish that you could have been here to see them men with their papers meet half way and exhange papers. I think that thare was fifty papers exchanged with our brigade in five minutes. Then they taken down their flags on boath sides and went to shooting again. There is a regular fireing kept up on boath sides night and day. Only when the flags is up. The yanks will hollow to us sharp shooters in front to quit that shooting and they will. I belong to the sharp shooters of a night. We have to go out in front of our breastworks and shoot at yanks with our rifle. I have to stand guard every other night and that is all the duty that I have to do. I have nothing to do through the day at all.

On March 27, about a week after David wrote Nancy this letter, the Yankees ran his regiment out of Petersburg. They were marching on the road to Five Forks the next day when a group of Yankees came out of nowhere and began shooting at them. During the skirmish that day, David was shot in the right thigh. He was taken to Jackson Hospital in Richmond, Va., along with several other soldiers who had been wounded. He was in severe pain, but wanted badly to write Nancy and tell her what happened, but he had no paper.

On April 3, General Grant took over Richmond and stormed the hospital, taking all the wounded Rebels as Prisoners of War.

Infection had set up in David's leg, and he couldn't be moved. Guards stood over him night and day. But it wasn't like he was going anywhere. He was in and out of consciousness. His pain worse than anything he had ever suffered. A kind nurse would come to him two or three times a day to change his bandages. At times, when he looked at her, he could see his Nancy. The long, dark hair, the chickipen eyes and the small figure just reminded him of what he had left behind. He wished so badly to have a picture of Nancy to look at, but he only had the memory of her etched in his mind. He would slip into a deep sleep where he would hold Nancy in his arms and make passionate love to her. In his dreams he could see her, feel her, even smell the scent of her body. Then he would wake, screaming in pain.

For 10 days he suffered, until a man clad in white took his hand and told him they would have to amputate his leg. He begged and pleaded with the doctor to find another way. He would never be no good to Nancy without his leg.

"Please just wait," he said to the doctor. "I need a piece of paper! Has anybody got a piece of paper?" he screamed as he lost consciousness again.

In his dreams he was at home on the mountain. His children were gathered around him laughing and giggling at a story he was telling them. His Nancy was cooking and it smelled so good. She was humming to herself as she fried chicken over the fire, the large Dutch oven full of taters and onions. He grabbed her by the dress tail and pulled her to him, kissing her soft lips as she sat down in his lap. Never had he been any happier in all his days.

He awoke to the nurse dabbing his head with a wet cloth.

"I have some good news," she said, smiling down at him. "General Lee surrendered five days ago. The war is over in Virginia. That means it will soon be over everywhere, even down south where you come from."

David was so weak he could barely speak. "I need paper," he said. The nurse leaned over and put her ear to his lips so she could hear him. "I need paper," he said again. "My Nancy. I need to tell her I'm comin' home."

"It's ok," she whispered. "I'll try to find you some paper so you can write to your wife. But you need to lie still."

He was fighting for his life. His body began to convulse. He couldn't breath. It was like his entire being was on fire. He was gasping for air as the nurse tried to calm him down. All he wanted was a damn piece of paper. He had to get Nancy a letter. He had to tell her how much she meant to him. He had to tell her ... he faded out again.

And this time, on this day, April 14, 1865 -- he never came back.

A commotion started in the hospital. Everyone was talking and running around as if they didn't know what to do next. The soldier lying in the bed next to David called out, "Will somebody tell me what's goin' on! Somebody! Anybody! What's goin' on?"

"Lincoln's dead!" someone yelled. "President Lincoln's been shot."

The soldier looked over in the bed beside him where David's body lay. A single tear ran down his cheek. Oliver Carson had been through a lot with David. He considered him a friend. Now the war was over, the president was dead, but David would never know it. That soldier would never go home, and all he wanted was a piece of paper.

He called the nurse over to him and asked her if David had any belongings on him when he came in. He wanted to take what he could to David's family on his way home to Yancey County.

"He didn't have anything," she said, as she pulled the sheet over David's face. "He talked about his wife, but he didn't even carry a likeness of her with him unless he lost it in battle."

Oliver lay back in his bed. He couldn't believe that soon it would be all over and he would be going home. He was overjoyed and sad at the same time. How many soldiers, like David, had fought through this entire war only to never go home.

News traveled fast to the cove. Nancy was cutting out rows in her garden to plant some peas when she saw old Silas McCurry coming up the road. She leaned against her hoe and watched. He was almost running and she wondered what his hurry was.

When he caught sight of her, he started waving his old hat and yelling, "Did you hear, Nancy? Did you hear? The war is over!"

Nancy stood in silence as he came closer to her. He was out of breath and she just knew she had heard him wrong.

"It's over, Nancy. Your man a be comin' home soon. They all are comin' home soon." He was grinning from ear to ear as he laid his hand on her shoulder. "You alright, Nancy?"

She felt weak. She dropped the hoe and grabbed hold of Silas to keep from falling to the ground.

"Is it true? David's comin' home for good?"

She just couldn't believe it. She had yearned for him for so long and now it was finally over. They could have their life back. Before she realized what she was doing, she had her arms around old Silas and they was hugging and laughing and dancing right there in the middle of Nancy's muddy garden.

Then the church bell started ringing. The only time that bell had rung since the war started was when word came to them that one of

149

their own had died. Then, someone would ring it 12 times, and all would mourn the loss. But today the bell had a different ring to it and as Nancy and Silas watched, folks from the cove, mostly women and children, started making their way toward the church.

Nancy's children came running into the garden. They were all excited because they knew something good was happening. All Nancy could say as they gathered around her was, "Pa's comin' home! Your pa's comin' home! The war is over!"

They laughed. They cried. They wanted to know when he was coming home. Then they all gathered at the church with the neighbors to thank the good Lord for ending the war and bringing the men home.

It would be several weeks before Nancy would see the first soldier walking up the old road. But it wasn't her David. She hadn't heard a word from him, but still she watched. Day in and day out, she watched the road for any sign of him. Several times, she would think it was him, but it would be someone else, either from the cove or passing through on his way home. They all looked starved and worn out. But she had no extra food to give them. She asked one after the other, "Do you know David Parker?" Some of them didn't know him, some of them knew him but didn't know where he was.

Nancy tried to busy herself with the garden and the children. More than a month passed and she was nigh on in to the end of her pregnancy. She hoped that David would be home in time for the birth of the new baby. She watched and waited.

Finally, one evening as she sat in the old rocking chair on the porch, she saw a man in a tattered uniform limping up the trail. She sit and watched as he neared the house. She felt the tears welling up in her eyes and her heart began to pound as if it were coming plumb out of her chest. She knew before he even told her, but still she listened.

"The names Carson ma'am, Oliver Carson. I was in winter quarters with your husband," he choked up, when he realized Nancy was with child. Then he cleared his throat and continued. "He was a good man. All he wanted was a piece a paper to write you a letter." He sank to the steps unable to go on.

Nancy sat in the chair, rocking back and forth, trying to take it all in. For three years her David had fought the war because he thought it was his duty. For three long, hard years her and the children had been starved and shoeless at times. For three years she had wanted nothing but for him to come back to her. Now he was gone. When the war was all over, he was gone. She cupped her hands over her face and cried like she had never cried before. David had given her the only real happiness she had ever had in her life. How could she live without him? How on earth would they survive? They had nothing.

Oliver went to Nancy and put his arms around her and let her cry while he told her what had happened to David. "He loved you Mrs. Parker. More than anything in the world he wanted to come home to you. He begged fer paper to write you in the hospital, but nobody had any to give him. He'd lose consciousness and holler out your name," he paused. "I think they buried him in Hollywood Cemetery in Richmond, Virginia. That's where they put 'em all that died. I'm so sorry fer your loss, ma'am. He was a good man."

There was nothing more Oliver could say. He stood, put his tattered gray hat back on his head and walked off the porch and down the trail, leaving Nancy to her sorrows.

151

She was numb. She couldn't, for the life of her, bring herself to move. She just sat and rocked, back and forth, back and forth. There were so many things going through her mind, but the one thought she couldn't get a hold of was the one that told her she would never see her David again. He would never hold her in his arms again. He would never see his children again. He would never even know he had another child. Oh, how she wished she would have told him. Maybe then he would have stayed with her.

Little Bill came out on the porch to see if there was anything for supper. He took one look at his ma and he knew. He ran off the porch and into the woods. Nancy didn't go after him. She knew he would have to deal with it in his own way.

Then Charlie and the girls came out. Nancy gathered them around her and they all cried. How on earth was she gonna make it?

"Why'd you have to go and take him so soon?" she prayed out loud, her face turned up toward heaven. "Why'd you have to take him atall? We needed him God. We needed him more than you!"

She was angry at God. She was angry at the world. She was alone. Even with her children around her, she had never felt so alone.

When daylight broke the next morning, Nancy knew she had to find the strength to carry on because of the children. If it weren't for them, she would have just laid down and died herself. Over a breakfast of syrup poured over dried apples, she told the children she wanted them to stay home with her 'till they got the cornfield planted. The girls could continue to go to the neighbors if they were needed, but the boys would stay with her and work the fields.

Within a couple of days, everyone on Cane Branch knew that David wasn't coming home. Some of the men who knew him, and had returned from the war, offered to help her. But they all had their own farms to get ready and she couldn't be a burden on them.

She and the boys had about half the cornfield planted when William K. Robinson came calling. She knew who he was, for he had delivered some of David's letters to her. She also knew he made moonshine somewhere on Cane Branch, or at least he did before the war started.

She stood with her hands on her belly and watched as he made his way across the field. "Evening ma'am," he said, tipping his dirty old hat to her.

"What can I do fer you?" she asked.

"I'm sorry to hear 'bout David," he stammered. "He was a good man."

"He was," she said, never taking her eyes off William. "But I'm sure that ain't why you're here."

"Well, actually I was thankin' you might need some help with this here field."

"And, just what makes you thank that?"

"Looky here," William said, wiping the sweat off his brow with his handkerchief. "I ain't here to cause you no trouble. I was just a wonderin', maybe if you don't need all this here field, we could work somethin' out sos I could have part of it."

"And just what are you thinkin' about workin' out?" Nancy asked bluntly. She knew William was a bootlegger and she didn't quite trust him yet, but she was willing to hear what he had to say.

"Well, ifen you let me have half the field to plant in corn, I'll either give you some of the corn or I can pay you for it."

"And just how you plan on payin' me for it? Ain't nobody got no money."

Her David had always been against hard liquor, swearing and playing cards. He would never allow her to make such a deal with the likes of this man.

"Now, Mrs. Parker, you know what I do for a livin'. Everybody in this here cove knows. Now that the war's over, I need to get back in business and I need plenty of corn to do that. Now I'm askin' you if I can have half this field and I'll pay you for it somehow. You know my word is good."

Oh how she wished David was here. If he was here, she wouldn't even be having to consider such a thing. She knew that she had to do something to take care of her children. Right now, she had not one penny to her name and she would need money come fall of the year. David would just have to forgive her for this one, she thought as she told William that she would take him up on his offer as long as he could pay her before winter. He agreed, they shook hands, and he left her alone to finish her work.

Actually, she was glad she didn't have to plant the rest of the field. She was tired and the boys was tired. Now, she could put all her energy into her vegetable garden and fruit trees and not have to worry so much about the cornfield.

Warm weather reached Cane Branch early and for that Nancy was glad. The only thing she had to look forward to was the birth of her baby and the vegetables coming in so they wouldn't be hungry. William got the other half of the cornfield planted and it was just day by day living for all them. Yes the war was over, but times were harder now than ever before. Folks had took to stealing from each other just to survive and Nancy knew that, sooner or later, it would come to her. She lived on the mountain and her garden was down next to the road. She tried not to worry. Maybe everybody was scared enough of her not to bother her stuff. But fear was something people put aside when they were hungry. Nancy had even thought of stealing a chicken or two from the old man that lived just across the hill, but had decided against it, afraid she would get caught and they would mark her as a thief. That was all she needed to go along with her reputation. Try as she may, she could never escape the fact that her mother had murdered her father. Through the years she had tried to put it behind her, but occasionally, she couldn't resist taking the long, dark strands of hair from her old trunk and running them through her fingers. She wondered what her mother and father was like. She wondered if they loved her at all like Grandma Stewart and Granny Silver had always told her. There were many times she needed her mother so badly. She had no one. No one to tell her troubles to. So she just bared them all by herself.

It was the hottest July Nancy could ever remember. She supposed it was because she was pregnant. She had intended to spend the day in the garden hoeing out the weeds, but the heat was just too much for her.

Before she made it back to the house, the pains started. She sat down on an old stump and hollered for Bill. She had birthed five babies already, so she wasn't scared, she just needed to get to the house.

Bill and Charlie came running from the garden and helped Nancy to the house. She told Bill to harness up the old mare and ride into Burnsville to get Aunt Sinda. Bill did as he was told, while the girls tried to make her comfortable. She told them to sit quietly and think of names for the new baby. Then she waited.

Shortly after noon Bill came back with Aunt Sinda. Nancy knew it was getting close and with each pain she thought about David. She wished he could be there with her. She wished she would have told him about the baby.

Finally, Sinda sent the children outside. It was time. She hummed a lullaby as she busied herself boiling water and making a bed in the wood box for the baby to lie in.

A couple of hard pushes and Cansada Parker came into the world, July 29, 1865. Nancy held the naked baby close to her breasts and wept. They were tears of joy, sadness, fear and heartache that ran down Nancy's cheeks that day.

Aunt Sinda sat on the bed and cried with her, cradling them both in her big arms and rocking back and forth. "Po' little Nancy. My old fool heart's jest a breakin' fer you child," she said.

Aunt Sinda was always there for her and Nancy knew it as Sinda took the baby and told her to get some rest.

Nancy drifted off into a deep sleep where David was holding her in his arms and telling her how proud of her he was and how beautiful the baby was. But his eyes were sad, just like she knew they must have been when he took his last breath. All he wanted was to come home to her and the children, but instead, he had left them all alone.

Nancy woke to sunshine pouring through the cracks in the wall. It was a new day and she had a lot to do. She was weak as she tried to stand and Sinda was quick to tell her not to be in such a hurry. She didn't have to be back at the inn until that evening so she would take care of things till then. But Nancy would hear nothing of it. She had just had a baby, but she was a tough mountain woman and things like that didn't keep her down. She busied herself throughout the day with Cansada and the other children until Sinda had to leave.

The boys tended the garden while the girls helped with the baby and Nancy was back and forth. There was plenty to do. There were trees to cut for wood, vegetables to pick and put up, fruit to dry, corn to pull and syrup to make.

Nancy had figured on having a good stand of green beans and had been waiting until they were just right for picking. That morning she made her way to the garden and stopped short of the bean patch. It looked like a bunch of wild hogs had been rooting around in it and there wasn't a single bean left on the vines. Her heart sank to her feet. "How could anyone do this," she thought. She had worked so hard to keep her family fed. Anger boiled through her blood as she took a deep breath and thought of David. If he were here he would say, "Now Nancy, we'll just have two good pickin's instead a three. We'll be fine, you'll see."

She closed her eyes and thought of those words until she calmed down. She would just have to figure out a way to watch the garden day and night, and right now the only way she could do that would be to move back to the little shack. So she made haste and gathered the cucumbers, tomatoes and squash and went back home to ready her and the children to move.

The next day, they began toting things down the mountain to the shack. The children loved the shack, so they were excited. When they got to the bottom of the mountain, Nancy looked toward the cornfield, and once again, her heart sank to her feet. Someone had helped themselves to the corn. She immediately sent Bill with word to William. It was one thing to mess with her crop, but it was another to mess with William K. Robinson's crop and, to her knowledge, no one knew the agreement the two of them had together.

William was fit to be tied when he seen that someone had wiped out several rows of his corn. Nancy told him that her and the children were moving back into the cabin and he assured her that he would be watching at night to see if he could catch who was stealing their crop.

Nancy kept the old shotgun loaded, standing beside the door. But no one came. Word must have gotten out in the cove, and whoever it was never came back. Nancy only hoped they choked on her green beans when they ate them. How dare someone take food from the mouths of her children.

By the end of October, all the harvest was in. Everything they could get their hands on was stored in the cellar or buried in the ground. William had made the promise of some money before winter set in, but as times would have it, there was no money available until he could get a run of whiskey into Georgia, hopefully in December if weather permitted. Still he kept his promise to Nancy and brought her two laying hens and a young pig he was raising. Nancy was excited at the thought of having a little meat for the winter and fresh eggs, but she still needed cloth and leather, which she had hoped to buy with the money.

The only thing Nancy could think of was to take two of her quilts to Vester Mitchel's store in Burnsville and see if he would be willing to trade with her. She had enough quilts to keep them warm through the winter and could even patch them if need be.

Old man Vester wasn't in much of a mood to bargain. He had been hit hard, too. There still wasn't any trade going on between the North and the South. Most all the railroads had been destroyed and would take some time to build back so his supplies was very limited and he had to make a living too. He wasn't even getting much from the South because the Northern troops had came through and burned out large farms and fields, destroying everything in their path. And what they didn't get, Kirk's Raiders got. Many men had been killed in the war, leaving much of the land unattended and farms crumbling to the ground for lack of having someone to take care of them. He figured it would be a long time before things got back to normal, and money would be worth what it had been before the war. With all this in mind, he finally agreed to take one of the quilts in exchange for a bolt of cloth and enough leather for one pair of shoes. Regardless of Nancy's disappointment, he assured her that he was doing her a favor by even allowing her that much for one quilt. All the women quilted, and he doubted if he would ever be able to get anything for hers.

She really wanted to have the luxury of some real coffee, but that wasn't of importance at that time. She had boiled chestnut hulls in place of coffee for awhile now and even though it was sometimes bitter, at least it was free.

She had also hoped to purchase more leather as she thought about how she had to tie bark on the kid's feet last winter for shoes. "Just maybe," she thought as she left the store, "I could take the other quilt to Miss Lucy at the inn and get something I need in exchange."

Aunt Sinda was glad to see Nancy out and about and led her into the inn where she asked Lucy if she had anything she would be willing to trade for the quilt.

"Well, now, let me see here," she studied the fine stitching in the quilt. "I surely could use an extra quilt. Would you be willing to take some leather in exchange?"

Nancy's eyes lit up, "I'd be mighty proud to take some leather. Then I could make shoes for my younguns."

"Well, I had a gentleman stay in a room about a week ago. Paid me in good leather, but I really have no use for it," Lucy said.

Nancy felt good as she made her way back home with the goods. She now had enough leather to make three pairs of shoes. She figured she could make one pair for the boys to share. She would make them to fit Bill, but Charlie could wear them too, they would just be a little big for him. She would do the same for the girls and then make herself a pair with what was left.

She would make what clothes she could out of the material, also making them to fit the bigger kids, but they could share them with the smaller ones as well.

Cold weather hit Cane Branch in full force by the end of November. Temperatures dropped and snow began to fall that evening. By morning there was more than an inch blanketing the children's covers where it had blown through the cracks in the wall that night. In all her haste to get everything done for the winter, she hadn't thought about it coming on this early. She would have to get back up on the mountain before they all froze to death in the little shack.

The wind howled through the rafters night and day as Nancy and the boys tried to keep a fire going in the fireplace. She put straw in the bottom of the wood box and covered it with some old wool she had to keep Cansada warm. The others sat as close to the fire as they could get, rotating from front to back trying to stay warm.

After about three days, the wind finally settled down and the snow stopped. By then, Nancy couldn't even push the door open on the old shack. She opened the shutter in the back and pushed Bill through to the snow-covered ground, where he could fetch the shovel and dig them out. Then she and the boys strapped on the old snow shoes she had made the first winter David had left her and made their way up the side of the mountain to the cabin, where they built a fire. Little Charlie's feet were numb by that time. Bill had on the new shoes Nancy had made and Charlie was still wearing the ones with holes in them and no sole except for a piece of bark tied around them. So he stayed with the fire while Nancy and Bill went back to the shack to gather their belongings.

Once Nancy was sure the cabin was warm, she set out to get them moved back. First, she took the girls, one at a time, carrying them on her back up the steep mountain slope. Then, she began carrying the few belongings they had. It would be several days before they were settled in for the winter, but at least the cabin had a floor and there were no cracks in the wall, for David had chinked the old logs with mud when he built it.

Temperatures continued to drop. The spring was frozen over, so they had to break the ice up and melt it over the fire to even get water to the animals. No way could Nancy lose her horse or her milk cow, and she had hoped to keep the pig alive till it got a little bigger, but, if she had to, she would go ahead and kill it.

It was getting close to Christmas, and she wondered what had happened to William. She had not seen a single soul in over a month. She had no way of hearing any news or gossip. All she knew was that her and the children were surviving, and she wanted badly to do something for them for Christmas.

She found a couple of forked sticks from a tree and she had a couple strands of leather left that she had planned on saving, but instead

161

she decided she could make the boys a slingshot with it. After the kids would go to bed, she would take some of the worn material she had saved to patch quilts with and make each of the girls a doll. She was pleased that, for this Christmas, they would have something special from her.

Then William showed up. He was on his way into Burnsville when he stopped to give her some money from selling his first good run of moonshine. She was so excited, she could hardly contain herself. He gave her five dollars and a promise of more later. She asked him if he would bring back some stick candy for the kids for Christmas.

She carefully tucked the treasures away in her old trunk and waited for the holiday. It was all she had to look forward to as each day was such a struggle. Snow continued to cover the frozen ground and temperatures dropped below zero.

Two days before Christmas, she bundled herself up as best she could and made her way outside to feed the animals. One of her chickens lay on the ground dead. It had frozen to death while roosting in a tree that night. The other one was near dead. She didn't even move when Nancy took her off her perch and carried her inside the shed with the other animals. She would pluck the other one and have him for Christmas dinner.

She walked a short distance into the woods with her ax until she found a small sapling. She chopped the little pine tree down and carried it into the house. Before David had left them to go to war, he had always cut them a small tree to decorate for Christmas. But while he was gone, she just hadn't had the time or energy to do such a thing. Now her children needed a tree. She needed a tree, just to prove to herself that there was still a bit of normalcy in their lives.

That Christmas was one that would stand out in Nancy's memory for many years. David was gone, and she wished with all her heart that he could be there with them. She tried to make up for his loss by cooking a good meal and giving the children the gifts she had made them. Aunt Sinda was there as usual, and it was the best day she had had since the last time David was home.

CHAPTER ELEVEN
1866–1869

Things were hard on Cane Branch, but they were just as hard all over the country. Nancy and the children survived another winter and things were beginning to look up. Old man William continued to bring her money on occasion. It wasn't much, but it was enough to keep them fairly clothed and shod. He was the only help she had, outside of her children and Aunt Sinda. No one else in the cove wanted anything to do with her, and that was fine. She liked the seclusion, and she liked being by herself.

She let William have half the cornfield again, just so she wouldn't have to plant it herself, plus that was the only money she had coming in. But, long about December, a man by the name of Edward Boone came calling.

He was from Burnsville and was interested in leasing some property to farm. Aunt Sinda had sent him her way, knowing that she could use all the help she could get. Nancy and Mr. Boone walked over the property and talked about how the lease should be taken care of. He was a smart man, soft spoken and Nancy liked him.

A few days later, he returned with papers he had gotten drawn up at the courthouse. The papers stated that she would agree to lease to Edward Boone "all the farm south of the calf fence that is on the ridge between the two fields dividing the calf pasture North of the building and garden and the field at the barn and also do agree that said Boone has the liberty of farming and clearing as much ground as he pleases and to have the ground he clears three years rent free and garden and potatoes patch and tobacco patch rent free. Boone shall have all the farm for four years or otherwise forfeit the sum of two hundred dollars for each year. Boone agrees to repair the fencing and building and pay to Nancy another part of all the grain raised on said old ground and one third part of all new ground after three years from clearing and further agree to gather the corn in three piles and give said Nancy choice of piles and of such wheat as ripe to be stacked in the shock. Boone will haul and stack all the small grain for Nancy and put good fences round said stacks in the field. Boone agrees to leave the terms of the lease of the farm at the end of this five years in good repair or otherwise forfeit and pay the sum of one hundred dollars for failure."

Mr. Boone read the lease agreement to Nancy. She listened intently rolling its terms over in her head. She would be a fool not to take this man up on his offer. Seemed to her, he would be doing all the work and she would be reaping much of the benefits.

December 18, 1866, Nancy signed her name to the lease with Edward Boone.

The only thing she hadn't contemplated was the fact that there would be no actual money coming in from the lease. She would have to bank on Charlie and Bill to compensate with work they could pick up in the cove, and perhaps Sinda could get her some sewing to do for folks staying at the inn.

Things went well until early spring. For sometime now, Nancy had been having problems with her teeth. Major sickness had evaded her and the family and for that she could be thankful. But she knew it was time for her to visit the dentist before she wouldn't be able to eat anything at all.

Nancy didn't feel much like walking, so she harnessed up the old mare and rode into Burnsville to visit Dr. McHorton. She had nothing to trade him or no money to give him, he would have to just take her word that she would pay him when she got it.

Dr. McHorton was used to such financial agreements. For the most part, he took his pay in eggs or vegetables. Nancy had neither to offer, and he could tell she was in much pain, so he agreed to a handshake and a promise of payment.

She left the office with a couple less teeth, but no pain, owing him one dollar and twenty cents. She had no idea how she would come up with the money, she could only hope that something would come her way.

For several months, nothing was said. Then one day in July, Nancy was in the garden when she saw a horse and buggy coming up the road. She stopped and leaned against her hoe, wiping the sweat from her neck with her apron. As the buggy drew near, she recognized Dr. McHorton.

He tipped his black hat to her, then told her he had come to collect his money.

"My apologies, sir," Nancy said, dropping her head in shame. She had never owed nobody in her life and felt extremely bad that this man had to come all this way for his money. "You know times is hard and I just ain't got no money to pay you yet."

"I understand ma'am. Truly I do. But I need to make a livin' too." He was sincere. He hated worse than anything to have to call on people for payment.

"I understand that too sir. I promise I'll git you some money jest as soon as I can," Nancy said. And she meant it. She just didn't know where the money would come from.

All he could do was tip his hat to her and ride off. She didn't offer him any vegetables for payment or he may have considered taking something to that effect. He would give her a little more time, then he would come back.

She hated to take the few cents the boys made here and there to pay for her teeth and she just wouldn't do that. She did, however, use their pennies to buy salt or things that was of a necessity to them.

When all her vegetables came in, she contemplated paying the dentist with her goods, but then decided against it. For the last five winters, they had struggled so hard to survive, nearly starving even when there seemed to be plenty to start with. She just couldn't risk taking food from her children to pay a debt. There would have to be another way.

December brought the dentist back to Cane Branch once again. Only this time, he threatened to law her if she couldn't pay.

"I would be willing to take payment in the way of canned or dried goods, if you'd like," McHorton offered.

Nancy would hear none of that, instead she said, "I could give you a quilt me and the girls made." It was more of a question than an answer and she waited for his reply.

"I'm sorry. Really I am," he said. "But I have no use for a quilt."

All she could do was, once again, promise to have him the money as soon as she could. But soon was not good enough for the dentist.

After he left, she started to thinking about what would happen if he did indeed take her to court. She didn't have anything. Even her property wasn't solely hers. When she married David the property automatically went into his name. After his death, without a will, she was only allowed the same share as her children. So technically, she only owned one seventh of the property, her six children owned the rest.

'It's like everything else in this godforsaken land," she thought. "Women have no rights whatsoever."

How in under the sun would she be able to fight for what was hers? Legally it wasn't hers to begin with and her children were too young to fight for anything. All she could hope for was that it had been an empty threat from the dentist.

But it wasn't.

On January 10, 1868, the sheriff came knocking on Nancy's door with a piece of paper stating that she was to appear at the Burnsville Courthouse on January 15. She read the summons out loud trying to take it all in.

"Are you goin' Ma?" Bill asked in excitement. "I can go with you ifen you want me to."

"No, I ain't a goin'," she answered angrily. "What good would it do? A woman cain't even testify in a courtroom full of men folk and if she could, they wouldn't listen to her anyway. I ain't got nothin' to say to any of 'em."

"But Ma, won't you git in trouble if you don't go?" Bill asked in concern.

"What are they gonna do Bill, put me in jail? I don't thank they would do that." At least she hoped they wouldn't, but at this point, she had no idea what they would do to her. She just wished everybody would leave her alone.

January 15 passed and she didn't go to the courthouse.

A week later the sheriff showed up again with another summons for the spring term.

Nancy took the piece of paper and read it carefully. Then, as the sheriff looked on, she tore the paper into pieces and threw it on the ground, stomping it in the mud.

"Now, Mrs. Parker," the sheriff started.

"Don't you Mrs. Parker me," she said, staring him square in the eyes. She put her hands on her hips and stood her ground. "You can bring me all them there papers you want to and that still ain't gonna get no money outta me, 'cause I ain't got none. And I ain't goin' to no courthouse to tell everybody that, 'cause it ain't nobody's business."

"But Mrs. Parker," the sheriff started again.

"I said what I had to say sheriff. Now you can take your white ass on down the road 'cause you ain't gettin' nothin' from me and you can tell that Mr. McHorton the same thang. I ain't got no money I tell you. I ain't got nothin' atall."

The sheriff knew there was no use arguing with Nancy. He understood that she didn't have anything, he was just trying to do his job. He could sympathize with her, but he couldn't help her, so he turned his horse and left.

Nancy was fighting mad. How dare they keep begging her for money they knew she didn't have. She was just mad enough now, that even if she had the money, there would be no way in hell she would give it to the likes of them.

Again, she did not show up for the spring term, and again, the sheriff came calling with another summons for the August term.

This time, before he even handed her the paper, he told her that it was very important that she read what the summons said.

"I cain't help you," he said to her. "But you should know that a court cost has been added to the amount you owe the dentist."

Nancy didn't say a word as she took the paper from the sheriff. Sure enough, a court cost of $7.75 had been added to the dentist fee, making the total $9.95.

She never said a word. Instead, she walked in the house and took the shotgun down from over the fireplace. She walked back out on the porch and pointed it straight at the sheriff, who hadn't even bothered to get down off his horse.

"I done already told you once, that I ain't got no money," she said. "Now git off my property and don't you come back."

"Mrs. Parker, please just listen," he said calmly, trying to reason with her. But Nancy would hear nothing of the sort.

She pulled back the hammer on the gun and took aim, "I said git off my property and don't come back a botherin' me no more."

The sheriff knew she meant business. There was nothing he could do but leave. She sure was a feisty little woman, he grinned to himself as he rode down the mountainside and headed back to Burnsville.

"What's a goin' on Sheriff?" a man called out as he reined his horse in beside the sheriff.

The sheriff recognized David Silver immediately. He was the son of Greenberry Silver, but he wasn't at all like his pa. He was always poking around in other folk's business and the sheriff didn't much like him.

"That Mrs. Parker up on the mountain there owes some money to a dentist in Burnsville and she cain't pay the bill. I keep havin' to bring her papers for court and she keeps gettin' all fired up over it. Just doin' my job," he told David, hoping he hadn't said too much.

"Is that right?" David asked. Immediately he started thinking. He was Nancy's second cousin, and he was as mean as she was. Her great uncle Will Griffeth left this land to her daddy. David's daddy had never had a problem with Nancy getting the land after her daddy was killed. But as David grew up and got an understanding of how it had all come about, he resented Nancy, and felt like she should not have gotten anything after what her mother did. He had never liked Nancy, and figured that he might could use this information to get this property back in the Silver family where it belonged. And he knew just the right person to help him.

Will Griffeth had left all his property on Cane Branch to his nephews on his wife's side of the family, the Silvers. J.O. Griffeth was a nephew, but he wasn't a Silver, so he didn't get any of the property. David had known J.O. all his life and knew the man held great resentment toward Nancy. So David rode straight to see J.O. with a plan. He could pay off the money Nancy owed and say that she had signed a deed turning her property over to him in exchange. J.O. would sign the deed as a witness to her signature X. They would record it at the courthouse before Nancy even knew what was going on.

J.O agreed to the plan only if David paid him. This was a problem because David was like everybody else, he didn't have much money. He had enough to pay off Nancy's debt, but he didn't have enough to pay J.O. the twenty dollars he was asking for. But he knew somebody who did.

David's sister was married to Golden Edge. They also lived on Cane Branch and their property butted up to Nancy's. David went to their house with his plan and to ask Golden for the money to pay J.O.

Nancy's David had been a good friend to Golden. But he was gone now and everyone was hitting on hard times. No one seemed to care about anyone but themselves. The war had pretty much destroyed

172

any trust between neighbors and friends. Golden figured Nancy would make out just fine. She could take her children and go live with some of the Stuarts someplace else and they would be rid of her and all her trouble-making for good.

Golden agreed to give him the money, but only if he could have the larger part of the property.

"We'll go straight up the creek," David said. "I'll take the 30 acres on the left side. You take what's on the right side, about 70 acres."

All David really wanted was the house and barn, he didn't care who had the rest of the property as long as it wasn't Nancy.

They shook hands and met with J.O. the next day. Golden gave him the 20 dollars, they made the deeds and signed Nancy's name with only an X, and J.O. signed his name beside it as a witness. They decided they could claim the property after the August 1869 court term if Nancy still hadn't paid.

Nancy didn't show up for the August court date in 1868 and hoped that would be the end of it. She didn't hear nothing else about it until a year later when the sheriff returned to Nancy's house with another summons to court. Nancy didn't even bother to get mad. She had most of her property leased out to Mr. Boone anyway, so what could they do if she didn't show up? She took the paper, thanked the sheriff and slammed the door in his face.

After the August court, Aunt Sinda was in the kitchen at the inn when Golden and David came in for a cup of coffee. She didn't mean to be nosey, but she couldn't help but overhear them talking about how Nancy didn't show up in court again, so they went and paid the bill for her. At first she thought they were being nice, but she should have known better. They started talking about recording a deed of some sort and how surprised Nancy was gonna be when she realized what they had done, and there was nothing she could do about it.

"Good Lord," Sinda thought. "Shorely they is not gonna do that to that po woman and them children." She quickly took off her apron and went out the back door. She had to get to Nancy and tell her what was going on.

By the time Sinda got to Nancy's, she was out of breath and sweating so badly there was not a dry spot on her.

"What in blue blazes brings you here in such a hurry?" Nancy called from the porch when she saw Sinda rushing up the trail holding her skirt tail up.

"Nancy, I's got somethin' to tell you and it's mighty bad Nancy. It's mighty bad," Sinda said breathlessly.

Nancy got up from the rocking chair and went to Sinda. "Slow down and catch your breath for you die on me right here."

Nancy helped her to the porch, fetched her a dipper of cold water, then asked, "Now, what is it that's so bad you need to tell me?"

"Well, I's be workin' in the kitchen when these two men comes in fer coffee," she began slowly. "I weren't listenin' in, no sirree, I wasn't. Least not till's I hear yo name mentioned."

"My name?" Nancy asked in surprise. "Who was it a talkin'?"

"It be David Silver and that Golden Edge," she said. "I hear 'em a sayin' they been to the courthouse to pay yo doctor bill."

"They did what?" Nancy was even more surprised. "Why on earth would they do that for me? Ain't nobody ever done anythang like that before."

"Just wait, that ain't all," Sinda said, lowering her eyes to look at the porch. "They's gonna take yo property Nancy. All of it."

Nancy jumped to her feet. "Like hell they are," she shouted.

"Now Nancy, sit on back down there," Sinda said, trying to calm her down. "We just gotta thank about this and figure it out."

Nancy was pacing back and forth, rubbing her hands on her apron. "They can't take my land," she thought. "Not legally anyway." She had to get to the courthouse and see what was going on.

The next morning Sinda and Nancy made their way into Burnsville. Nancy carried the lease between her and Mr. Boone with her, just in case. She hated worse than anything to have to be doing this. She knew she would have to stand her ground or anything could happen. She was a widow woman with six children. Her husband had been well respected in these parts, but she hadn't. And now she had to face a bunch of highfaluting men and try to explain to them that she was just trying to make a living and she had no money and someone else held a five-year lease to her property, though it had not been recorded as of yet at the courthouse.

She held her head high when she walked into the big building. It was a scary place for her and she really didn't want to be there. None the less, she had to do what she should have done a long time ago.

She approached a man in a suit, told him who she was and asked him where she needed to go to record a lease. He led her to an office, where he set down behind the desk and told her he was the one she needed to talk to. She handed him the lease agreement with her signature on it. He read it over carefully, then asked her why it had taken her almost three years to bring it in.

"I just had other thangs to do, that's all, and I didn't thank it was that important," she said. "Me and Mr. Boone been gettin' along just fine. No trouble atall. Then I caught wind of somethin' that made me thank I needed to get this done properly."

"And what might you have caught wind of?" the clerk ask her.

"I was sposed to have been here for court yesterdy for a debt I owe the dentist. I didn't come 'cause I ain't got no money to pay him. But I heared somebody paid the debt for me and I don't know why."

"Well I can check on that for you Mrs. Parker," he said. Leaving the room.

Nancy was nervous, but she tried not to show it.

A few minutes later the clerk came back in and told her that, yes indeed, the debt had been paid in full. "Maybe whoever paid it just wanted to do something nice for you," he told her.

"Ain't nobody ever done nothin' nice for me mister," she said. "I just keep thankin' they gonna want my property or somethin' in return."

"Well now Mrs. Parker, let's make sure your property is still your property," he said. He smiled at her, trying to comfort her. She was a mountain woman through and through and he could tell she was uncomfortable.

He left the room for a few minutes, and returned to tell her that nothing had been recorded concerning her property. For that she was relieved, but she still wasn't sure what was going on. The more she thought about it, the more confused she became. But, one thing was for sure, nobody, not one single person that she could think of, would ever pay off a debt for somebody and not want something in return.

176

"Just take it as a good deed," the clerk interrupted her thoughts. "There's still good folks out there."

Nancy just didn't believe that. She had known very few good folks in her lifetime, and though most of them were dead, the ones still living had managed to get on her bad side.

She walked home, wondering the entire way what was to become of her and the children. It was times like this that she missed her David the most. He had always been so good at figuring stuff out. She, on the other hand, had gotten used to just living from day to day, and that's what she would have to keep doing.

She made her way to the cabin and set down in the rocker totally exhausted. Then she made up her mind that nobody would take what was hers without a fight. She may not know how to fight them in court, but she damn sure knew how to fight like she had done all her life. She would lay low and keep her ears open for a spell. She knew David Silver was as mean as they come. She knew he was probably laughing at her right now. He was going to get his revenge on Frankie Silver one way or the other, and she knew he didn't give one red cent what happened to her or the children. Golden, on the other hand, had surprised her. He and her David had been friends. For the life of her she couldn't understand his motives against her, except that he was married to a Silver. Nancy knew she would carry the burden of that last name with her for the rest of her life.

For two weeks Nancy kept her ears open, but never heard the first thing. Of course there wasn't much she could hear when the only people she really came in contact with was Mr. Boone and old man Robinson. She had told them what she suspected of David and Golden, but neither of them had heard anything about it. They assured her that no one could take her property as long as it was under lease and Sinda must have just misunderstood the conversation at the inn that day. Just when she was beginning to believe them, the sheriff came riding in again.

Nancy wanted to run, but knew she had to stand her ground for whatever it was he was bringing her this time -- and she knew it couldn't be good.

Mr. Boone met the sheriff at the road, followed by Robinson. They exchanged a bit of conversation, then they all turned to look at Nancy.

"I ain't got nothin' to say to you sheriff," Nancy hollered to him across the field.

He got down off his horse.

"Come here Nancy," Mr. Boone said. "There's somethin' you got to hear."

"I ain't got to hear anythang," she said, still not moving.

"Nancy, you have to hear me out, this is important," the sheriff said, approaching her.

Nancy started backing up. "I'll git my gun, sheriff. I mean it. I told you not to come back on my property ever again."

"Come on Nancy," old man Robinson said. "You have to hear what he has to say."

Nancy stopped, trying to consider her options. It didn't take her long to figure out that she had none. She had absolutely no choice but to hear him out.

When the sheriff got to where she was standing, he handed her a piece of paper. "You cain't tear this one up Mrs. Parker. It won't do no good. It's what we call an eviction notice and it says you have 30 days to get off this property, because it now belongs to someone else."

"That ain't possible," Nancy said, taking the paper from him. "Boone here says as long as he has a lease on my property, ain't nobody can take it from me."

"Technically, that would be true. But according to this notice, it looks like, in February of this year, you signed your land over to a Mr. David Silver. I don't know why he held it, but it was recorded yesterdy, September 27, at the courthouse."

Nancy's hands began to tremble. "I did no such thang," she said, almost in tears.

"It's right here," he said, handing her the papers. "Signed with your X and a witness."

"But why would I sign these here papers with an X and not my own name?" she asked. "I can write my own name. And I couldn't sale my property to nobody 'cause of that lease with Mr. Boone."

"All I can tell you, " the sheriff said, "is you'll have to prove what you're sayin' in a court of law and it would be your word against David Silver's."

Nancy felt defeated, but she wasn't through yet. "It all comes down to us women's rights," she said, her voice raising. "And we ain't got any."

"Now hold on Mrs. Parker," the sheriff started.

"I owned this property clear on up 'till I got married. Then the law says it belongs to my husband," she yelled at the sheriff. "Well that ain't fair. Then when he goes and dies on me, I don't even git the land back in my own name. I only git one share of it, just like my younguns. You see, I cain't sale or give all this land away, 'cause it ain't even all mine. Now since you men are so damn high and mighty, hows 'bout tellin' me how all this works, 'cause for the life of me, I cain't figure it out and if I cain't figure it out, then how the hell is the court gonna figure it out without makin' me look like the bad person, which always happens to a woman in court."

"I don't know Nancy," the sheriff said, lowering his eyes. He felt so ashamed, just because he was a man and he knew what she was saying was right. But there was nothing he could do about it. "I'm sorry ma'am. I really am. I'm just doin' my job here. All I know is you will have to fight it in court."

"But court cost money," Nancy said quietly now, "and I couldn't even pay a dollar and twenty cents to the dentist. If I coulda, I wouldn't be in this situation to begin with, now would I?"

Mr. Boone and old man Robinson just stood and listened. Even they couldn't believe what they were hearing. How could any man, if he were a man at all, run a window with six children off her property? It was unheard of and they would try to figure out a way to help her.

Nancy was spent. She had no more argument left in her. She turned to walk away and the sheriff called after her. She stopped, but didn't turn around.

"Remember, 30 days or I'll have to come back and arrest you, and I really don't want to have to do that," he said.

"How could I forget," she mumbled under her breath.

As she walked off, Boone and Robinson ran to her. There had to be something they could do. They couldn't just stand there and let her lose everything she had.

"Nancy," Boone said, taking her arm. "Stop for a minute, and let's figure this out."

Nancy stopped and looked at him. Tears welled up in her eyes. "Seems to me there ain't nothin' to figure out, Mr. Boone. Least not with me, anyway. Guess you'll have to take your lease up with David Silver now."

Old man Robinson's blood was a boiling. He had lived in these parts all his life and he knew the story of Frankie Silver. He knew how everybody looked down on Nancy because of her mother, and it just wasn't fair. He had watched how she had struggled to take care of her children the last few years. He had seen how tough she was and now he was seeing her defeat. It made him want to go to David Silver's house right this minute and beat the living daylights out of him.

Nancy got to the shack and set down on the edge of the porch. She was thinking hard about what she would do when Bill came running in. He stopped short when he saw the three of them there.

"What's goin' on?" he asked, his dark hair hanging in his eyes from underneath the hat his father had given him years before. It was old and worn out, but Bill just couldn't let it go. It was the only thing he had left of his pa.

Nancy looked up at her boy. He was 17 years old now and had grown into a fine young man. She couldn't help but think how much he looked like her David. She reached up and took his hand in hers. "We have to leave, Bill," she said.

"What do you mean leave, Ma?" he asked with concern.

"We have to go away. The farm ain't ours no more."

"But I don't understand. If it ain't ours, then whose is it?" he questioned.

"Don't matter whose it is. It ain't ours and we have to go."

"But where will we go?" Bill was on his knees beside her now. He just couldn't believe what he was hearing. This was the only home he had ever known and now he was gonna have to leave.

"Ma, where will we go?" he asked again.

Nancy was thinking. There was only one place that she knew she could go.

"To Ellijay," she answered. "We'll go to Ellijay to our Stuart relations."

Bill had often heard his mother talk of Jacob and Elizabeth Stuart. They had even come to see them once when Bill was little. He knew they had raised his mother until she was five years old and went to live with her grandma. Even though Jacob and Elizabeth were dead and gone now, their daughter, Lidia, and her husband, Abe Moore, still lived there.

"But how will we get there Ma? Ain't it a long way to Ellijay?"

"It's a long way to Macon County, Bill. We'll just have to figure somethin' out."

"I did hear tell of a wagon train leavin' outta here in a couple days headed that direction," Boone said. "It'd be tough to get ready in such short notice, but it'll be the last one out before winter sets in."

"But Ma, we don't even have a wagon," Bill said.

"I do," old man Robinson spoke up. Nancy had almost forgotten he was there. "I could loan you my wagon."

"But we only got one horse," Bill said.

"I could loan you a horse, too," he said, pulling up a blade of grass and sticking it between his teeth.

"I cain't do that," Nancy said.

"Seems to me you don't have a choice," Robinson told her. "Look, if it'll make you feel better, I'll send my boy, William, with you. He can bring the wagon and the horse back in the spring. I don't need him through the winter much anyhow."

"But he may not want to go, and I shore wouldn't make him," Nancy said. "We'll find another way."

"Now see here," Robinson said sternly. "I'm a tryin' to help you, if you'll let me. The boy's 21. He ain't got no woman, he ain't go no job, so there ain't nothin' keepin' him here 'cept me and his mammy. He needs to get out and see the world. So it's settled then. You hear?"

Nancy knew Robinson was done and there would be no more arguing about it. She had seen his boy a time or two when he helped in the cornfield. He was nice enough, and she could use the extra help to handle the horses and wagon.

That evening Nancy gathered the children around the fireplace and told them what was going on. She told them to get a good rest, because at first light the next morning, they would be loading up the wagon and heading into Burnsville. They were all there except Margaret Alice. She had gone over the ridge to stay with a little girl that she had made friends with in church. Nancy had let her go for a few days, seeing as how the harvest was almost over and she felt like the children needed to be children every now and then and not have to work all the time.

That night she lay in bed thinking. She knew that a wagon train would not be easy with one wagon and six children. They would have to take enough food to carry them over and a few belongings to set up housekeeping with, once they got there. Nancy knew the trip was a five-day trip with one wagon, so she figured it would take them at least a week with the wagon train. She thought about everything she had put her children through, and she suddenly felt an overwhelming sadness. It was so unfair to them that they should suffer anymore because of her. She had struggled so hard to keep them clothed and fed since the war. She had worried about them day in and day out. She was so afraid of losing them, that she may have unknowingly kept them from anything to do with society. She wanted them to go to school and have friends. She wanted them to grow up and have children of their own. She didn't want people to hurt them, like she had been hurt all her life.

That's when she decided to leave Margaret Alice behind. She was with a family that Nancy knew could take care of another child. A family that she knew could provide better for Margaret Alice than she herself ever could.

How dare she think such thoughts? Nancy couldn't believe that she was actually thinking of giving up one of her children. Why, David would roll over in his grave at such an idea. But it would be better, she tried to convince herself. It would be easier on Margaret Alice and it would be easier on her. That would be one less mouth to feed, one less to make room for to sleep in the wagon, one less for her to worry about, because she knew that Margaret Alice would be safe where she was.

Nancy tossed and turned all night, until daylight finally broke. Old man Robinson was already at the barn with the horse and wagon. His son was there too, just itching to go on the wagon train with them. They worked for hours, bringing stuff from the cabin. She brought her old trunk, which held her beloved David's war letters and her mother's hair, along with bed clothes. She also brought the old cook table that her grandmother had given her when she and David came to Cane Branch. The table had belonged to her mother, so Nancy just couldn't

184

leave it behind. She gathered up all the canned and dried goods that the wagon would hold, along with several quilts she and the girls had made.

It was late afternoon before they were finally ready to go.

"What about Margaret Alice?" Rhetta asked. "We cain't leave without Margaret Alice!"

Nancy turned to Rhetta and said, "Yes we can Rhetta. Margaret Alice will be fine where she is 'till spring, then we'll come back and git her."

"But Ma," Bill stepped in. "We cain't just leave her without even sayin' goodbye. That ain't right."

"We can and we are," Nancy said sternly. "We ain't got no choice 'cause we ain't got time to go fetch her. I'm tellin' you, she'll be fine. I'll send word by old man Robinson to go and tell her we'll be back in the spring."

Tears welled up in Rhetta's eyes, "But Ma, she's only 10 years old. She won't understand. She'll thank we ain't a comin' back."

"She'll understand," Nancy argued. "I promise you she will. Now let's go, all a you. It's time to go."

The children knew there was no arguing with their mother. They would leave their sister behind and there was nothing they could do about it. Nancy herself was fighting back the tears as she and Bill slapped the horses with the reins and headed off down the road. She knew she was doing the right thing, but it still tore her heart in two.

"Bill," she said. He didn't look at her and she knew he was mad. "First sign of spring, you'll come back for your sister, you hear?"

He didn't say a word, but kept his eyes on the road in front of him. He did hear, but all he could think about was how Margaret Alice would feel when old man Robinson told her that she was to stay where she was until spring. She would think that none of them wanted her, including him.

Nancy turned and looked at the other children walking beside the wagon with William Robinson. They all walked with their heads down and the girls were wiping at their eyes. She knew they were crying over their sister. She held Cansada on her lap and even she looked sad, though she wasn't old enough to know what was really going on.

Nothing else was said as they continued on to Burnsville and met up with the rest of the wagon train. They left at first light the next morning, headed in the direction of Macon County. Nancy took turns riding in the wagon seat with the girls so they wouldn't have to walk the entire way and Bill, Charlie and William took turns at the reins.

Four days later, while they were camped at the foot of Balsam Mountain in Haywood County, the wagon master came into Nancy's camp bringing word that one of the families in the wagon train had the smallpox. He had moved the family as far back as possible from the other wagons, and they would be traveling far behind at morning. Smallpox was a very contagious disease, and Nancy felt sick to her stomach at hearing this news. The way she figured it, there were only six wagons in the entire group and one of them was filled with sickness, so the odds were surely against the rest of them. She made sure the children knew to stay close to their own wagon until they got to Scott's Creek the next day to get help.

Nancy kept a close eye on her children throughout the night. Any sign of a rash on them would tell her if they were sick, even before a fever set in.

Morning came and the wagon train made their way on into Scotts Creek in Jackson County, where the wagon master went and fetched a doctor. Everyone watched and waited for the doctor to check out the sick family and inform them on what they should do next.

After only a short time, the doctor gathered them all around him and told them that all three children and the mother and father had the dreaded disease. He informed them that it was in the best interest of the community to quarantine all of them right where they were, until all symptoms of the disease had passed.

They were all in a panic as the doctor told them to gather up all their blankets and bedclothes and wash them in boiling water, and to not be anywhere near the sick wagon until he returned in a few days to check on them. "If you want to help the sick, you can take them food, but you should leave it settin' someplace where they can come out and pick it up without you being in contact with them," he said. "This is a very contagious disease and the best way not to get it, is to stay as far away as possible from those who have it."

Nancy instructed Bill and William to take the wagon and the horses as far out in the pasture as they could get. All the other wagons did the same. Then they all waited.

Three days later, the doctor returned. There was no good news as he came from the sick wagon, except that no one else had contacted the disease.

A few days later, the mother's wails could be heard coming from the wagon and they all knew that she had lost a child. They watched as the father carried a small bundle from the wagon and laid it on the ground.

On his knees beside the bundle, he called out to them across the field to help him bury his baby. The men took shovels from the wagon and made their way across the creek to Locust Field Cemetery, where they dug a small grave. Then they all watched as the father carried the bundle to the grave and cried as he covered it with dirt.

The next two days, one by one were carried to the cemetery in the same fashion until only the father remained when the doctor returned. Nancy and the others were hoping he would let them move on, but he would not hear of it. It would be too risky to let them pass through Sylva carrying the disease. So he ordered them to stay.

While Nancy and the others waited to move on, she was unaware that back in Burnsville, on November 1, Golden Edge was recording a deed he had allegedly made with her for 70 acres of her land. He hoped she never found out that he had taken part in running her off her property. David Parker had been his friend and Golden knew if he were still alive, David would never forgive him for what he had done.

Another month had passed. Food was getting slim and everyone on the wagon train was more than ready to leave. Nights were getting colder and already a dusting of snow had fell. Finally, a couple weeks before Christmas, the good doctor returned to tell them it was safe to journey on. No one else had contacted the disease and the father had completely mended. It was time for them to go.

The wagon master led them from Scott's Creek, over Cowee Mountain, into Macon County. From there, Nancy and her family made their way to Ellijay. They traveled along the Cullasaja River and, as Nancy listened to the wooden wheels turn, she closed her eyes. It seemed like forever ago that she had traveled this same path with Jacob and Elizabeth. She was young, but she could remember it so well because she was scared. Now here she was coming back and she was still scared. She had sent word to Abe and Lydia from Scott's Creek that she was coming, but had not heard anything back.

The children were excited and anxious to get there. They had grown tired of the wagon, sleeping on the ground and eating beans and cornbread. They were ready to settle into a new home. William was even excited. He and Nancy had grown quite close while on the wagon train. He was almost half her age, but much more of a man than she had anticipated.

He and Bill had taken good care of the horses, helped the other men in the wagon train and spent much time hunting and fishing to keep them in food. He had almost became a father-figure for the girls and, sometimes, she would catch him watching her. She would smile at him and he would smile back. It had been so long since she had let a man hold her that she had almost forgotten what it would be like, but, more and more, she found herself thinking about William. Then she would laugh to herself and think what a silly notion that was. He was young and good looking. It was just a matter of time before a sweet, young lass swept him off his feet. But, she had to admit, she liked the attention.

She was shaken from her thoughts as they came to a stop at the ford of the river. She and William would take the wagon across with the girls in back, then he would go back and get Bill and Charlie, as the water was too cold to wade in.

This was the last leg of their journey. She stood on the bank, watching with her girls, wondering what Margaret Alice was doing right now. She had spent many restless nights worrying over what she had done, but at the same time, convincing herself that it was the right thing. Before long, they would go back and get her, and they could all be a family again.

Nancy was amazed that not much had changed in Ellijay that she remembered. When they got to Jacob and Elizabeth's old home place, where Nancy had spent the first years of her life, she thought about how happy she had been and wished her grandmother would have just left her there. Jacob and Elizabeth had been wonderful parents to her. She stopped the buggy in front of the old house and closed her eyes. She could almost hear Elizabeth's sweet voice singing her to sleep as the katydids hollered in the cool night air. They had written each other often through the years, hoping that, someday, either she could come back here to live or they could come to her. But neither happened. Still, she knew they had never stopped loving her, and she had certainly always loved them. If it weren't for them she, no doubt, would be living amongst the Silver family and there wasn't a single one of them that she cared much about. They had always been too quick to blame her mother for all the bad things in their life, and even now, it continued. She could hardly stand the thoughts of David Silver living in the house her David had built for them, claiming the property that was the only thing she had ever owned in her life. They had taken it all and left her to start over again. She sure hoped they were happy because she was finished with them all, and they would never have to look at her or her children again if she had anything to do with it.

She coaxed the horses past the house a short distance. She could see smoke coming from the chimney and, for the first time since leaving Franklin, realized that she was cold. The front door opened, and there was Abe and Lydia, a bit older than she had expected, but arms open ready to meet her and the children.

A Christmas tree had already been trimmed in hopes that they would arrive before the holiday, and the house was warm and cozy.

"We ain't got much room here, Nancy," Lydia said kindly. "So, I hope the children will be comfortable on the floor."

"That's fine," Nancy said, looking around the rustic old cabin.

"You can sleep in the loft."

"That's fine," Nancy said again.

"Look," Lydia smiled, taking Nancy by the arm, "I know this is hard for you. But life ain't always easy. You know that yourself. If you'd like, you can fix up Ma and Pa's old house and you and the children can live there as long as you like."

Nancy didn't answer.

"Our children are all grown and have their own homes. That one's just sittin' there, and I know Ma and Pa would want you to have it. They loved you Nancy."

Nancy tossed and turned all night, thinking about how her life had changed in such a short time. The next morning, Abe and Lydia walked with them down to Jacob's old house and they talked about what they would have to do to get it ready to live in.

Then Abe took Nancy by the arm and told her he had something else to show her.

"I don't know if anybody ever told you or not where your ma's buried," Abe said to her, leading her through the field a short piece and into the woods.

"Not really," Nancy said. "Granny Stuart always said that Granddaddy was so worried about somebody diggin' her up, that he made three or four different graves so nobody would know for sure where she was buried."

Abe stopped and pointed to a small clearing in the woods where several rocks stood. "Right there she lays," he said quietly. "Jacob and Elizabeth lay beside her."

Nancy dropped to her knees, her hands covering her face. "You mean all this time she was here. Even when I was a little girl and lived here?"

"All this time, Nancy," Lydia said.

"You see, Nancy," Abe said, laying his hand on her shoulder, "your granddaddy was right in his thinkin'. Folks have searched for her remains for years. But while he was a diggin' all them graves, Frankie was in the back of me and Jacob's wagon, headed back here to Ellijay."

Nancy got up and made her way to the stones. Abe pointed out which one belonged to Frankie, and Nancy reached out and touched it, ever so gently, almost as if she were touching her mother's face. Tears streamed down her cheeks as the children gathered around her and she told them again what had happened to her ma.

All of this was so hard for her. She just didn't know what to do next. She had never thought her life would be this way, and she was angry. She was angry at David for dying and leaving her to raise their children. She was angry at her mother for taking away her pa. She was angry at the law for taking away her mother, and she was angry at herself for leaving Margaret Alice behind. But more than anything, she was angry at God. She felt like he had forsaken her. But in her heart, she knew that she should be thankful to God for giving her a place to come to. She would make the best of it and live day by day like she always had -- and somewhere along the way, she would find peace.

CHAPTER TWELVE
1870–1872

That winter sure was a cold one up on Ellijay, but the children were content and so was Nancy. She and William and the boys worked hard to get Jacob's old house fit enough for them to live in. As they worked, she and William talked -- for hours on end it seemed. Nancy found herself telling him things that she had never spoken of except to her David. William knew the things he had heard about Nancy's mother, but she told him her side of the story and how she had came to live here when she was a baby.

One day as they worked, the snow began to fall outside. Nancy pulled her shawl around her shoulders and walked out on the porch of the old house. Already, the trees were glistening with frozen frost. The branches of the hemlock tree in front of the house were almost touching the ground and two turtle doves pecked at the earth underneath searching for something to eat. The air was as crisp as fresh linen hanging on the clothes line, and the quietness, tucked in amongst these mountains, was a stillness one could only hear if they were there. The picture sent chills up and down Nancy's spine.

She hadn't heard anyone come out of the house until she felt his hands slip under her shawl. He wrapped his arms around her and kissed her neck. She closed her eyes, and, for a split second, she faded away.

"What the heck!" she yelled, coming to her senses. She pulled away and turned to face William.

Before she could say another word, he pulled her into his arms and kissed her tender lips. She tried to pull away again, but he held her tight to his manhood.

"You know you want it as bad as I do Nancy," he said to her.

"But I cain't William, you know better than that," she whispered.

Oh, but she wanted him too. She had been lonely for so long, that the very inside of her hungered for the touch of a man.

"All I know is I want you and I want you right now," William muttered between kisses. He kissed her lips. He kissed her neck. Then his fingers made their way to the buttons of her dress.

"I cain't," she said, pulling away breathlessly. "Not here, not now. What about the boys?"

William had been so lost with passion he had forgotten about Bill and Charlie in the house. Nancy was right, this wasn't the right place or time, but he had made his move and he knew that, before long, she would be his.

"You're right," he said, rubbing his forehead sheepishly. He shoved his hands in his pockets and looked down at his shoes. "Sorry, Nancy. I just couldn't help myself."

She straightened up her dress with her hands. "It's ok," she said, touching him gently on the arm as she brushed past to go inside.

She shut the door and leaned against it. Her heart was pounding and her cheeks were hot. What on earth was she thinking? She couldn't get caught up with the likes of William. Her own boy was almost his age. But he wanted her, and she hadn't had anybody want her in a very long time. But it was just a moment and she knew it would pass. He would be leaving come spring anyway to take his pa's horse and wagon back home. She would have Bill ride with him to bring Margaret Alice to Ellijay, where she planned on staying for awhile. She had no place else to go and she would send the younger girls to school from here, if they wanted to go. Her David had always wanted them to have an education.

"Ahh, my David," she thought. If only those could have been his lips touching hers and his hands caressing her. But it wasn't, and she knew she would never feel him again. She brushed her thoughts to the side -- she had other things to do besides getting all fancy with a man anyway.

As she busied herself with the house and the children, she would catch William watching her. Sometimes she could feel her cheeks burning red and she would have to turn her thoughts away from him. He didn't approach her again and for that she was glad -- or was she? At nights she would lie in bed trying to get her mind on other things, but more often than not, she would relive the day on the porch. It would pass eventually, but only when he went away. She knew once he went back to Cane Branch she would probably never see him again, so it was best just to leave it alone.

Warm weather was finally touching the mountains, and Nancy was ready to move into her new home. Jacob and Lydia had given them more than enough hospitality and it was time to get out from under their wings. They carried their few belongings to the house in the wagon, while Bill and William prepared to travel back to Cane Branch. Nancy was excited. She knew that it wouldn't be long now till she would see Margaret Alice again. She had written to her several times, but had heard nothing back. So she had written Aunt Sinda asking her to check on Margaret to make sure she was alright. But she had heard nothing back from her either.

She had left Burnsville without even saying goodbye to Aunt Sinda. It had all happened so fast that she hadn't even thought about it.

Sinda was the only true friend Nancy had ever had. She had helped her through the hard years of the war. She had kept them from starving to death by bringing them scraps of food from the inn. She had defended Nancy to the end with neighbors and people of Burnsville. She thought perhaps she should go with William and Bill to get Margaret Alice. She was sure she could stay at the inn and have one last day together with Sinda. But she couldn't. There would only be one horse to come back on. If she went along then one of them would have to walk. She would have to find another way. Maybe one day she would make the trip alone.

At first light, Nancy wrapped a few biscuits and some cured pork in a cloth sack for Bill and William to eat on their trip to Burnsville. Bill was more than ready to go. He had been so upset about leaving Margaret Alice that he wished he would have just went and got her and then caught up with the wagon train. He would have done that if he had thought about it at the time.

William, on the other hand, was not ready to go at all. He had become totally infatuated with Nancy. He remembered the evening when they were camping at Scott's Creek. Nancy was cooking and William could see every curve of her shapely body through her dress from the warm red glow of the fire. It sent shivers up his spine to think about it. He had never been with a woman before, and he found himself wanting her so badly that he could hardly stand the throbbing in his groin. But he had taken his approach slowly, watching her, gently touching her hand accidentally on purpose, smiling at her when she was least expecting it. Nancy was tough. She had built a wall around her that William wasn't sure anyone could break, but he was sure enough willing to try -- and he had. It had felt like the right time on the porch that day, if only he had waited till they were alone. He knew she wanted him too, and here he was walking away from her.

Nancy came around the side of the wagon and handed him the cloth sack. When William reached for it, he wrapped his hand around hers and, for a moment, time stood still as they looked into each other's eyes. Then, quickly, she jerked away. She couldn't let him know what she was thinking.

"Nancy," he said, grabbing her gently by the arm. "I shore enough am gonna miss you."

'Damn," he thought. "Why can't I just take her in my arms right now? Why can't I just man up and do what I know we both want?"

"I'll miss you too, William," Nancy said. "You been a big help to me and the younguns and for that, I thank you."

William thought that was just too empty. It was as if she was talking to just anybody. He wanted more from her. He tightened his grip on her arm, "But Nancy."

Just as she jerked away from him, Bill came around the side of the wagon. "What are you doin' William?" he asked, knowing that he had walked in on something but he wasn't sure what.

"Just tellin' your ma bye, that's all," William said, looking at Nancy.

"Alright, you two need to get goin'," Nancy said, picking up her skirts. "I'm ready to see my girl."

As the wagon headed off down the road, Nancy watched. She wasn't sure what she was feeling. She was excited that Margaret Alice would be coming home, but she was sad that William would be gone. It was all for the best, she figured. She didn't need no man in her life anyway. She had made it this far by herself, she was convinced she could make it alone the rest of her life.

Bill and William rode in silence for awhile. Bill was trying to figure out what he had just saw between his ma and William, and William was trying to figure out how he could win Nancy over.

Finally, William broke the silence by telling Bill that he had taken a liking to Nancy.

"You what?" Bill shouted, shocked by his confession.

"I really have," William said. "I cain't help myself. She's a purty woman with that long, dark hair and those big, brown eyes."

"Now, hold on a minute," Bill said, angry that William would even consider such a thing. "That's my ma your talkin' about and she's too old for you anyways. And, the thang is, you ain't comin' back to Ellijay anyhow, so you just might as well forget any notions you have about courtin' her."

"But I been a thankin'," William said, ignoring the fact that he had made Bill mad, "I may just come on back to Ellijay, after I drop this here horse and wagon off."

Bill didn't know what to say. William was his friend and he liked him. He didn't like that he wanted to court his momma, but if he wanted to come back to Ellijay, Bill couldn't stop him.

"Well, all I gotta say is you better be good to her 'cause ifen you ain't, I'll shoot you myself," Bill said.

"You wouldn't do that now would you, Bill," William said, punching him in the arm like a schoolboy.

"I might just thank about it," Bill answered, his anger fading. He and William had become close since leaving Cane Branch, and regardless of how he felt about William and his mother, he would like it very much if he came back to Ellijay.

When they reached Cane Branch, they went straight to get Margaret Alice. She was in the yard playing with her friend when she saw them coming up the road. She ran to meet them. When Bill saw her, he jumped from the wagon before it even stopped, picked her up and swung her around and around as she giggled.

"Hurry up and go git your stuff together," Bill told her. "Ma's been waitin' months to see you."

The smile faded from Margaret Alice's face. "I ain't a goin'," she said.

"What do you mean, you ain't goin'?" Bill asked. He couldn't believe she would even say such a thing.

"I said I ain't goin' and you cain't make me," she said boldly.

Bill knelt down in front of her and took her hands in his. "Now Margaret Alice, you know you have to come home with me. You ain't but 11 years old, you cain't tell me what your gonna do. I came to fetch you home and I ain't leavin' here without you."

"Why not? You left without me before," she said, tears welling up in her eyes.

"But we had no choice," he tried to reason with her. "Look, I know you don't understand. But Ma did what she had to do. Now we're all settled in on Ellijay, and you have to come back with me."

"Well, they said I could stay here if I wanted to. They said they would send me to school and everythang. So I ain't goin'. I like it here, and Ma don't want me no how, so you can just go on and leave, Bill."

He didn't know what to say to her. He had never thought that she may not want to come home with him. Nancy would have a fit if he didn't bring her back.

So Bill just picked her up and threw her over his shoulder like a sack of potatoes. Margaret Alice went to kicking and screaming as he tried to put her in the wagon. Her friend, Sadie, ran into the house and came back out with her mother.

"Put her down this minute," the woman yelled to Bill.

Bill stood Margaret Alice back on the ground. The woman ran to her and told her to go inside that she would take care of this.

"Let her stay," she said to Bill. "She has a good home here and we have grown to love her. We'll take good care of her, and her ma can come see her anytime."

Bill felt defeated. "But that's my sister," he said, looking at the ground. "I cain't leave her again. I just cain't."

"Yes you can," the lady said. "It's for the same reason your ma left her. She'll be better off here and you know it."

Bill didn't say a word as he got back in the wagon. William didn't know what to say either. He knew Nancy would be devastated if Margaret Alice didn't come back with them.

"I promise she'll be alright," the woman said, turning back toward the house.

The two boys just sat there, waiting for Margaret Alice to change her mind. Then, when she didn't come back out, Bill pulled on the reins and headed the horses away from the house. Nary a word was spoken as they made their way to old man Robinson's.

This time it was Bill's turn to stay in the wagon while William told his pa that he was going back to Ellijay.

"What are you thinkin', boy?" his pa asked. "I need you right here. I been a needin' you bad to help with the business. If I'd a had any idear that wagon train would a been held up fer so long, I'd a never let you went to begin with."

William knew his pa was mad, but he was old enough to do what he wanted to and he wanted to go back to Ellijay.

As he unhooked the horses from the wagon, his pa begged him not to leave. Finally, William looked him square in the face and told him the truth.

"It's Nancy, Pa," he said. "I cain't leave her. She ain't got nobody."

"Well, I'll be damn," Robinson said, spitting a wad of tobacco on the ground. "You foolin' with that woman, ain't you boy?"

"No, Pa. It ain't nothin' like that," William said sheepishly, though he wished it was like that.

The old man put his arm around his boy. For the first time he realized William wasn't a boy at all, but had truly become a man since he had left last fall.

"Well, I happen to like that woman too," he said. "And yer right, she does need somebody to take care a her. I just never figured it'd be you. But I reckon that's alright. I just cain't believe you'd take a likin' to a hard headed woman like Nancy, and she's twice your age."

William couldn't believe it either. But he had took a liking to her, and now he just had to get her to feel the same.

He gathered up the few belongings he had, said his goodbyes, with a promise to come back and visit, and then they were on their way back to Ellijay with the one horse that belonged to Nancy.

When they came in view of the old house, they could see Nancy sitting in the rocking chair on the porch. Bill dreaded, worse than anything, to tell her Margaret Alice wouldn't come back with him.

Nancy heard them coming and got up from her chair. She was expecting to see Margaret Alice on the horse behind Bill, but what she saw made her heart drop to her knees.

Bill ran to his mother. "She wouldn't come, Ma. I tried and tried and she wouldn't come!"

Nancy sank back down in the rocking chair covering her face with her hands. Her sadness was overwhelming. It was worse than when she had found out that her David had died and wouldn't be coming home. This was her child, and she had left her behind. It was all her fault Margaret Alice hadn't come home. It was all her fault that she had broken the family up.

William knew this was the time. He went to her and wrapped his arms around her, letting her cry into his shoulder. The other children came out on the porch and, when they saw Bill and William, they cried, too.

"Is she dead, Ma?" nine-year-old Myra asked.

William took Myra's hand and said, "No, Myra, she ain't dead. She just didn't wanna come back, that's all."

"But why?" Myra asked confused. "Why wouldn't she wanna come back?"

"I don't know," Bill said, pacing back and forth. "That woman said to just leave her, that they could take care a her and send her to school. I guess she's just happy there and has more than we'll ever have on this damn mountain here."

Bill felt the anger building up inside of him. "It's all your fault, Ma! You should a never left her!"

He stomped off the porch.

"It's alright, Ma," Myra said, laying her head in Nancy's lap. "We can still go see her."

Nancy stroked Myra's dark hair as tears streamed down her cheeks. Then Retta and Cansada ran to her. "Yea, Ma," Retta said through her own tears. "We'll go see her. Then maybe she'll want to come home."

But she didn't. William took Nancy to Burnsville that summer to try and get Margaret Alice to come home, but she still didn't want to. Nancy knew she could have made her, but what good would that have done. She would just hate her even more than she already did.

"That little girl be happy right where she be," Aunt Sinda told Nancy when she went by the inn to see her. "I knows it be killin' your old heart, but you gots to let her go, Nancy."

"But I don't want to just let her go," Nancy argued.

"Then yous will just have to make her leave," Sinda said, spitting her snuff on the ground.

Nancy knew she had a choice to make. "Will you make shore she's took care of ifen I leave her?" she asked Sinda.

"You know I be more than glad to. I'm tellin' you, she be alright," Sinda patted Nancy's hand.

So they came home without Margaret Alice and tried to make the best of it. They had plenty to do. The field hadn't been planted since Jacob had died, so they had to clear it off first, then plant and hope the rains would come to give them a good crop.

They worked together downing trees and getting in wood for the winter. As they worked they talked about what they would plant and when they would harvest. They talked about making syrup and the people in Cane Branch. And, every now and then, Nancy would catch William watching her as she hoed or swung an ax to chop wood. He certainly had not forced himself on her, and she almost felt like he was waiting for her to make the next move. If that were the case, he would have a long wait, cause she wasn't throwing herself at no man for nothing.

The long summer days soon turned into fall, then cold weather reached the mountains of North Carolina. Nancy had finally put her old life behind her and moved on to a new life on Ellijay. She was content living here among her family. There was nobody bothering her about her past, 'cause nobody cared. When she did occasionally ride into town with the boys, no one stared at her or made fun of her because no one knew her. She was finally just where she wanted to be.

But on cold nights, when she crawled under the covers in her bed, she felt lonely. Those were the times when she would think about her David and Margaret Alice. She would even think about her mother and wonder if she would ever really know what happened to her pa. Then she would drift off to sleep wondering what else her miserable life held in store for her.

One night in January of 1871, she awoke to the sound of wind ripping the tin off the roof. Her quilt had a thin layer of snow covering it that had blown through the small cracks in the wall. She got up and made her way into the living room where William was putting more wood on the fire.

"It's bad out there," he said, pointing the fire poker toward the door.

"I know it is," Nancy said. "And it's freezin' in here."

She walked into the other room and placed another quilt over the girls, who were all asleep in the same bed. They had the warmest room in the house, next to the fireplace.

Nancy walked back to the fire and warmed her hands. Suddenly, she felt his breath on the back of her neck. His arms slid around her waist as he whispered, "I can keep you warm you know, ifen you'll let me."

She felt herself stiffen against his touch. But he didn't let her go. Instead, he pulled her tighter against him, till she could almost hear his heart pounding.

Her mind flooded with a desire that she had not felt since last winter on the porch. She had thought of that moment so many times and wondered if she would ever have another chance like that. Then, just when she thought he was gone forever, he had came back to her. She needed him and he needed her.

He felt her body relax as he turned her to face him. The fire flickered in the darkness of the room as he kissed her lips. Time stood still for an instant as the heat from their bodies warmed each other. Nancy could hear the wind whistling through the old hemlock outside, but she didn't care. She felt her feet leave the floor as William picked her up in his arms and carried her to her bed. He was filled with a passion like he had never had before, and she was filled with a desire to tame that passion.

Blizzard conditions wreaked havoc on Ellijay that night, but William and Nancy was oblivious to it all as they fulfilled the lusts within them until the wee hours of morning. Only when she heard the boys moving around in the loft, did she open her eyes and realize that she was laying in William's arms.

Quickly she jumped out of the bed. " You have to git up!" she poked at William. "The boys are awake!"

William didn't care. "It's alright Nancy," he said, his eyes heavy with sleep. He patted the bed next to him. "Git back in," he said playfully.

"I ain't a gonna do no such thang," she said, slipping into her old dress.

"Ma," she heard Charlie call out.

"Oh, dear Lord, I got to get out of here," she thought, scurrying into the living room.

"Looky outside, Ma," Charlie said from the window. "There ain't nothin' but snow out there."

Charlie was right. Snow had drifted against the house so deep that it covered the windows and the doors. It would be days before they could shovel themselves out.

About that time, William came out of Nancy's bedroom to see what all the fuss was about. By then all the children were up and they all turned to look at William as he buttoned his britches.

"What the hell are you doin' in there?" Bill asked, glaring at William.

"Now, Bill," Nancy started.

"Don't you Bill me, Ma! What the hell was he doin' in your room? Or has he been there all night?"

"Well," Nancy said, smoothing out her skirt like she always did when she was nervous. "I don't rightly thank that's any business of yourn, now is it Bill?"

She walked out of the room before he could say anything and William followed her. She had just had a wonderful, passionate night and there wasn't anybody going to make her feel bad for it. She wasn't sorry for what she had done. She was a grown woman and it was time the older children understood that. She didn't want to be alone anymore.

And she wasn't. That William Robinson followed her around like a whipped schoolboy till Nancy finally had to tell him to leave her alone for a spell. She was worried and William knew it, he just didn't know why. He could feel her stiffen up against him when he tried to hug her, just like she had done in the beginning. Sometimes she would even push him away and tell him, "not now." For the life of him, he couldn't figure her out.

It had taken them days to dig out from under the snow and repair all the damage to the roof and the barn. He tried to busy himself with all the work, leaving Nancy to herself, until he couldn't take it anymore.

He watched as Nancy sat rocking in front of the fire one evening, waiting for just the right time. Everyone else had gone to bed and it was as if she were in deep thought about something.

"What's on your mind?" he asked, breaking the silence in the room.

Nancy didn't answer.

He walked over and put his hand on her shoulder. "What's a botherin' you, Nancy?"

She covered his hand with hers and, without looking up at him, she said, "I thank we're gonna have a baby. That's what's a botherin' me. "

There was no excitement in her voice. There was no joy in her words. It was just plain and to the point.

William dropped to his knees beside her. He had a grin on his face a mile wide. He was so overjoyed he could hardly speak. "Are you shore?" he said.

Nancy turned on him then. "What do you mean, am I shore? Course I'm shore and I ain't none too happy about it either."

She was mad as an old hornet at him. How could she have let herself get so caught up in something like this? It was a wonder the children she had were still alive. One of them had done left her and here she was expecting another one. If he had just left her alone and stayed in Cane Branch when he went back, none of this would have ever happened.

"Well, I'm happy," William said gently. "I cain't help it if you ain't."

"How can you say that William Robinson, when you know what I been through my whole life? You ain't the one that has to carry it for nine months and you ain't the one to have to birth it and nurse it," she said angrily.

"I'll tell you one thang," William answered, getting to his feet and pointing his finger at her. "You'll love that baby just like you do the rest of 'em. You'll love it and you'll love me, too. You jest wait and see."

But she didn't love him. At least, not in the way she had loved her David. She couldn't even hardly look at him as a man; he wasn't much older than her own boy.

William took her hands and pulled her up in front of him. He looked deep into her eyes, wanting to see what he had saw the first night he took her as his. But what he saw was a deep, dark emptiness that made him feel sick in the pit of his stomach.

He let her go and stomped outside, slamming the door behind him. All he could think about was making her love him, when all she could think about was not loving him. He breathed in the fresh air for a long time until he felt the tension ease from his veins. Then he went back inside and crawled in bed next to her. He lay there looking up at the ceiling, not touching her, but wanting to hold her.

Sleep wouldn't come to neither of them. "You know we gotta git married," William finally said in the darkness.

Nancy didn't answer him. She knew that too. But how could she marry someone she didn't really love.

For months he tried to make her love him. He did everything for her and begged her to marry him. But for the life of her, she just couldn't find any feelings for him. He was good to her and the children. He was a fine worker, like she had never seen before. He provided for them as best he could, but there was still something missing.

Then folks in Ellijay started to talk. It was no secret that she and William had been messing around, but now she was beginning to show and the whispers started.

"Nancy, we have to git married whether you like it or not," William said to her one day. "Folks are talkin' and it ain't good. I ain't raisin' no bastard child. You hear me?"

Nancy knew he was angry and he had every right to be.

"I said, do you hear me?" He grabbed her by the shoulders and shook her roughly.

She looked him square in the eyes, anger building inside her. How dare he treat her like that. No man had ever laid a hand on her before and it wasn't about to start now.

She jerked away from him, planted her feet firmly and pointed her finger in his face. "Don't you ever lay a hand on me agin," she said. "I ain't ready to marry you now and I may never be ready to marry you. Let's get one thang straight here. I don't care what folks say, never have never will. They can talk all they want to, don't make no difference to me. I still ain't marryin' you."

He tried to reason with her, but it was no good. She was as stubborn as they come and he knew that it would just take some time, and he would have to be willing to give her that time.

Julius Commodore Robinson was born October 5, 1871. Lydia helped deliver him into the world and, as she lay him against Nancy's breast, it almost seemed he smiled. For the first time since he had been conceived, Nancy felt real joy as she looked down at him.

William had been pacing back and forth across the porch for hours. He was so worried about everything. Then he heard the baby cry. He listened for a minute or two. That had to be the sweetest sound he had ever heard. He couldn't stand it no longer. He busted through the door and stopped dead in his tracks when he saw Nancy holding their boy close to her, looking down into his eyes and smiling. He had not seen her smile for months, and he was overwhelmed. He went to her bedside and brushed the hair back from her face.

"Now, can we git married?" he said, grinning so big that Nancy couldn't help but laugh at him.

"We'll see about that," she said. "Now git on outta here and let me and this here boy have some rest."

He bent and kissed her on the cheek, leaving the room, content that she would indeed be his wife soon.

But Nancy put it off for four more months. She had one excuse after another for not marrying William. Truth of the matter was, she was scared. She was scared of losing him like she had lost her David. She was scared of being alone again and having to raise their child by herself. But most of all, she was scared of loving him.

Finally, she broke down and told him her fears.

"Seems I have a way a losin' people I love," she said to him. "I don't wanna lose you too. I ain't never been good at admittin' thangs like that, but it's the truth."

"Why didn't you tell me that before?" William asked.

"Cause bein' scared is a sign a weakness and they ain't a weak bone in me that I know of. I've had to be strong my whole life and it ain't no time now to be a scared. So, I reckon if gettin' married a make you happy, then we will."

"You mean it? You really mean it?" William was as excited as he had ever been. Already, Commodore was four months old and he knew folks were already calling him a bastard child. He knew Nancy still didn't love him like she ought to, but none of that mattered to him anymore. All he cared about was his boy and, once Nancy married him, it wouldn't matter how she felt.

It was January 10, 1872, when William hitched up the wagon to ride into Franklin to the courthouse. It was blustery cold, and the

211

ground was frozen solid. Nancy wanted to wait until spring, but William would hear no more excuses. Soon as the weather broke, 11-year-old Myrah and seven-year-old Cansada would be going to school and he didn't want anybody making fun of them because he and Nancy was unwed and had a baby together. He didn't care what the weather was, today was the day that he would take Nancy to be his wife.

They bundled up as best they could for the ride into Franklin. The hardest part would be crossing the Cullasaja River, and William hoped that it would be thawed enough for the horses to slosh through. They rode in silence through the twists and turns of the old road leading down Ellijay. Nancy knew she was doing the right thing, but, for the life of her, she just wasn't too happy about it. William was good to her and the kids. He had taken them in as if they were his own children and they loved him. Bill had gotten over his anger and had been courting Lucinda Moses, who lived on up Ellijay in the Mountain Grove settlement. That's where Myrah and Cansada would be going to school in the spring. Charlie was now 18 years old and Retta was 15, so both of them would soon be gone from home. But she would still have her little Commodore. It was like starting all over again, and even though she hadn't really wanted that, she was content with it all for now.

"Whoa," William called to the horses, bringing Nancy out of her thoughts. Already they were at the river and they had hardly spoken a word to each other.

William got down out of the wagon to check the river at the ford. The rocks were covered in ice and slippery, but he knew they would have to cross here anyway. It would be too risky to try and cross elsewhere. The water was frozen around the edges, but flowing rapidly through the middle.

He got back in the wagon and told Nancy to hold on as he cautiously led the horses across the water. Nancy held her breath as their hooves slipped and slid on the rocks leading into the river. The wagon felt as if it were about to turn on it's side. Then, steadily, they got into the running water and crossed the rest of the way without incident.

Once on the other side, Nancy breathed a sigh of relief.

As they made their way to the courthouse, Nancy was glad no one knew her. There weren't many folks out and about because of the weather. The ones that were only glanced their way, not caring why they had come to town.

Nancy felt numb standing in front of the Justice of the Peace, who was also the sheriff and the judge. He playfully told them they had two seconds to back out before he read their vows and pronounced them man and wife.

Nancy wanted to back out right then and there. She wanted nothing more than to lift her skirts and high-tail it back to Ellijay.

William looked at her and squeezed her hand. He knew what she was thinking, but she wasn't getting away from him that easy. He held her firmly and, five minutes later, they were leaving the courthouse a married couple.

"Dang it, Nancy, say somethin'," he said to her when they got in the wagon. "Do you even love me or is this just somethin' I made you do?"

For a minute, she didn't say anything. William searched her eyes for an answer.

"I reckon I love you," she finally said, turning to look at him. "I reckon I love you as good as I know how and if I wouldn't a wanted to marry you, they ain't no way you could a made me."

He sure enough knew that. She was one stubborn woman -- always had been -- that's one of the things he liked most about her.

"I got a quarter in my pocket, let's us go in here and see if that'll get us a piece a pie and a cup a coffee," he said, laying his arm across her shoulders. "I'm still a might cold and would like to warm up a little before we head back."

Nancy followed him into a small eating place where several men sat sipping hot coffee. Seemed like it hadn't been that long ago that she had yearned for a cup of the dark liquid, but there was none to be had. Now, seven years later, here she was drinking coffee and eating pie like it was the natural thing to be doing. But it wasn't. At least not for her. She felt uncomfortable as William chattered away at needless things while she watched those around her, wondering what they were thinking.

"How do you feel about that?" William interrupted her thoughts.

"How do I feel about what?" she asked.

"Dang it Nancy, do you ever really listen to me?"

"I listen, just not all the time."

"I was askin' you if you'd like to go see Margaret Alice in a few weeks, before school starts back."

"I'd like that," Nancy said. She hated it when William got aggravated with her. She wasn't afraid of him, but she still remembered the day he grabbed her and shook her, demanding that she marry him.

"Good," he said. "We'll do that and take the others with us, if they wanna go."

That night they lay in bed, both staring at the ceiling, till finally, William couldn't take it anymore. She was his wife now and, if he wanted her, he would have her.

Nancy didn't bother fighting him. She knew her duties as a wife. Maybe that was one of the reasons she hadn't really wanted to marry him. But it was too late for that now. She would just have to make the best of it and, if she really tried, she knew she could probably love him. He was a good man and she knew it. He would take good care of her and Commodore if she would let him -- and she would. She knew she would because she really had no other choice.

Come warm weather, they all went to Burnsville to see Margaret Alice and Aunt Sinda. They stopped at the inn first where Sinda came out to meet them, taking Commodore in her big, black arms and rocking him back and forth.

"I's missed you bad, Nancy. Why didn't you tell me you be havin' a baby and I mighta come and delivered the little feller for you."

"I figured it was too far for you to come and besides, we did fine," Nancy said. "Have you talked to Margaret Alice lately?"

"Seen that child just the other day," Sinda said. "Shore is a purty little thang. She be doin' fine, she is. Comes by to see me evertime she's in town."

She saw the sadness on Nancy's face. "You did the right thang, you know, leavin' her here and all. She wears them there nice clothes and is gettin' all her schoolin'. You did the right thang."

Margaret Alice had been gone from her for almost three years and Nancy's heart still felt broken when she thought about her.

"Maybe this time, she'll come back home with me," Nancy told Sinda.

"Yea, maybe this time," Sinda answered, knowing that she wouldn't but wanting to make Nancy feel better anyway.

They turned the wagon onto Cane Branch, and Nancy's thoughts went back to the first time she had seen this place with David. There was the little church and what was left of Aunt Sinda's cabin. The porch had fallen in and the roof was sagging. Briars and bushes had woven a tangled web across the front that you could hardly see through now. It had been a lively place back in the day when Nancy first saw it, smoke coming from the chimney and chickens pecking around in the yard.

Up ahead was the barn David built. The last time she was here, no one had been out and about, but today was different. Today she could see someone in the little garden in front of the shack. She took a deep breath, suddenly feeling sick to her stomach. She tightened her hold on Commodore.

William saw the man too, and turned to look at Nancy. He had seen that look on her face before and it wasn't good.

"It's over Nancy. Just forgit about it." He kept the horses at a steady pace as they neared the man.

Nancy stiffened when she recognized David Silver.

He looked up when he heard the wagon coming and leaned against his hoe, watching it as it got closer. "Well, I'll be damned, if it ain't Nancy Parker," he mumbled under his breath.

Nancy never took her eyes off him, though there was nothing she could do and she knew it.

When they got right up next to David, a grin came across his face and he hollered, "What the hell are you doin' back in these parts? Come to git that little girl back you left?"

Anger welled in Nancy's throat. She held Commodore in one arm and clutched the side of the wagon with her other hand till it turned white.

"Whose that man, Ma?" Cansada asked, tugging at Nancy's dress.

"It ain't nobody," she answered, still watching David.

But Bill knew who he was, and before David could say another word, Bill jumped out of the wagon and ran toward him yelling, "Don't you say another word to my ma or I'll kill you!"

David raised the hoe and swung, barely missing Bill's head as he ducked and grabbed David by the legs, taking him down in the middle of the garden. He was on top of David, pounding him in the face as he struggled to get up. William stopped the wagon and jumped out. Charlie was right behind him. William grabbed Bill and pulled him off David just as Charlie lunged, wrapping both hands around David's throat.

Nancy watched as William tried to get her boys off the man. He'd drag one off and the other would go after him, until finally Bill picked up the hoe and rared back, ready to strike David over the head.

"No Bill!" Nancy screamed from the wagon. "He ain't worth it."

Bill turned and looked at his ma. David squirmed in pain on the ground, covering his bloody face with his hands and knotting up in a little ball. Nancy couldn't help but feel pleasure from his pain. He had taken everything from her, driven her and her children off their own land, and now she would watch him beg for mercy.

"Put it down, Bill," Nancy said again. "You damned near already killed him, anyway."

"Yea, Bill, you damned near already killed me," David managed to say. "I ain't got nothin' against you boy."

"No, but maybe I got somethin' against you," Bill said. He was breathing hard and his hands trembled as he threw the hoe down right next to David's face. Then he reached down and pulled him up by his suspenders. David's eyes were already swelling and blood oozed from the side of his head into his ear. His lip was split open and he spit a mouthful of blood on the ground.

"Don't you ever say another word about my ma, do you hear me? Or, next time, you won't be so lucky." He slung David on the ground like a rag doll, leaving him to lay in his own blood. He walked back toward the wagon. William followed him, dusting the black dirt off his britches. Charlie stood looking down at the beaten man. He wasn't sure who he was, but he didn't like him. He kicked David hard in the ribs, before running toward the wagon. David screamed out in pain.

"Serves you right," Charlie said, wiping blood from his nose on the sleeve of his shirt.

"It sure enough does serve him right," Nancy thought as they rode away, leaving David lying in the dirt. Nancy didn't care if he lived or not. She didn't care about anybody in this cove except Margaret Alice. She would come and see her just as long as she was able. But she really wished she never had to come back here again. It was too painful for her, and she just wanted it to go away. If only she hadn't left Margaret Alice here.

But she had left her, and she would leave her again on this day, knowing in her heart that Margaret Alice would never, ever come to Ellijay. Her only prayer was that the rest of the children would never leave her.

Later that same year Bill married Lucinda. He built them a house up the road on Mountain Grove, promising Nancy to always stay close to her.

CHAPTER THIRTEEN
1879–1893

Seven years seemed to pass quickly in the Ellijay Community. William picked up his pa's trade of making moonshine, though Bill detested the idea. His own pa had been against drinking hard liquor, and so was he. Bill was an outstanding citizen of Ellijay, just like his father had been on Cane Branch, and Nancy couldn't have been more proud of him. She didn't like the idea of William making moonshine either, but it provided well for them, along with their crops and fruit trees.

Charlie married in the fall of 1877. Retta and Myrah went to school at Mountain Grove long enough to learn how to read and write, and little Commodore was preparing to start his first year there. They had all visited Margaret Alice a couple of times a year and she even came to see them on Ellijay once, but she would hear nothing about staying. As far as she was concerned her home had always been in Burnsville, and she was happy there.

Nancy made a good home for her and William. She had even grown to love him in a sense, but not like she had loved her David. William had been good to her and the children, but after Commodore was born Nancy had no desire to be with him intimately. On occasion, she had made herself fulfill her obligations as a wife, but William had been frustrated with her lack of passion. He was still a young buck. What had once drawn him to Nancy, had faded through the years. She had indeed had a hard life and, as age crept up on her, the lines of that life showed more and more on her face. Her long, dark hair had turned to gray and her chickipen eyes were lined with dark circles.

But when he looked at Myrah, he could see Nancy the way she had looked when he first set eyes on her. Myrah was the spitting image of her mother, and she had grown into a beautiful young woman. More and more, as Nancy pushed him away, his mind filled with images of 18-year-old Myra. He couldn't help himself. When they were working in the field and the sunlight glistened through Myra's dress, he could see every curve of her body and he felt himself wanting her in a way that no stepfather should ever want his stepdaughter.

William fought these feelings every day as he tried to fulfill his manhood with Nancy. If only she could see what she was doing to him. He had thought about finding him a willing woman elsewhere, but he had no choices in Ellijay.

One day, he and Myra were in the cornfield alone. The sun was hot for an April morning and seemed to beat down on them as they planted the corn. Beads of sweat formed on Williams forehead and he wiped them with his handkerchief. The front of Myra's dress clung to her breasts as she worked in the heat of the day. William watched, the throbbing in his groin lingering. He tried to fight it off as he continued covering the seeds that Myra dropped.

Myra never noticed William watching her. It was humid and she was content to get the job done so she could find some relief under a shade tree. With just a few rows left, she made her way to the edge of the field next to the creek. She took off her bonnet, bent down and wet the hem of her dress, then wiped her face with it. The cold water felt good, so she splashed it over her arms. She slid her dress up above her knees and stretched her legs out into the frigid water.

William watched from behind a tree till he couldn't take it anymore. He slowly crept up behind Myrah, startling her when he placed his hand on her shoulder.

"What the …," she started, but before she could finish the sentence, he was kneeling beside her with his hand run up her dress.

She tried to pull away from him, but he was too strong. She kicked the water as she slid off the rock backwards onto the soft ground under the trees.

"You know you want it as bad as I do," William said breathlessly, covering her mouth with his.

She bit his lip hard, bringing blood, but before she could scream his hand covered her mouth. She was fighting desperately under the weight of his body. She felt the twigs and rocks tearing the flesh from her arms and legs. Tears streamed down her cheeks as William tore at her dress with his other hand to expose her tender breasts. He was like a mountain lion, his eyes glazing red and wild as he found his prey.

Myra was more scared than she had ever been in her life. This was William, the man she had called Pa since she was a little girl. How could he be doing this to her? Her mind clouded with pain and she watched the leaves above her fade into the afternoon sun. The clouds moved and she could make out the head of a rabbit in one, 'til it slowly formed with another cloud to look like an evil demon with fangs and horns.

She jerked herself back to reality. She was laying on the ground, her dress torn and covered in dirt. There was no one else there, and, for a split second, she wondered if she had just imagined the whole thing.

Slowly she sat up, trying to grasp what had just happened. She crawled on her hands and knees to the middle of the creek, shivering in the cold, mountain water washing over her skinned up arms and legs. How on earth could she go home? How in the world would she ever be able to tell Ma what had happened? Would Ma even believe her, she wondered?

Myra sat on the creek bank until the sun was going down behind Onion Mountain before she headed across the field towards home.

Commodore was up in the old hemlock tree playing.

"Where ya been Myry?" he called out to her. "Ma's been a lookin' for you."

Myra didn't answer. She just kept walking, up the steps, onto the porch, through the old screen door, holding her breath in hopes that she could get to her room and change her dress before Ma saw her.

"That you Myra!" she heard coming from back porch.

"Yes Ma," Myra called out, reaching for the door to her room.

"Well get on out here girl and help me peel these taters for supper!"

"Be right there Ma," Myra answered, slipping into her bedroom and quickly changing her dress. She picked up the old hairbrush from the washstand and peered into the looking glass.

"Myra!" Nancy hollered again. "What on earth is keepin' you?"

Myra knew she had to face her mother sooner or later, so she ran the brush through her tangled hair and made her way out back.

Nancy took one look at her and knew something was wrong. "What in blue blazes happened to you?"

Myra didn't meet her mother's eyes, instead she looked down at the cracks in the rickety old porch. "Nothin' Ma," she said quietly, picking up a tater.

"Don't nothin' me," Nancy said, never taking her eyes off Myra as she sank back into the rocking chair.

"It ain't nothin', Ma," Myra said again. "I swear it."

But Nancy knew better.

They both sat quietly, for a time, peeling potatoes. Myra never looked at Nancy, but Nancy sure enough looked at her, all the time wondering what had her girl so upset. She didn't push her though, she knew that, eventually, Myra would tell her.

Nancy, Myra and Commodore ate supper in silence except for Commodore's occasional chatter. Then Myra crept into her bedroom, finally alone. She buried her face in her pillow and cried.

As night fell, William came home. Myra could hear him and Nancy talking, but she couldn't make out what they were saying. Her body ached and her head pounded, as she drifted off to sleep.

Light seeped in through the small window of Myra's room and she heard the rooster crowing in the distance. She sat up in the bed and listened.

"I said, I'll be back directly. I'm goin' to check my still if it's any a your business," she heard William say. His voice was raised and he seemed angry.

"Well, I was just a sayin' I need you to help me with the garden today," Nancy said.

"I reckon the damn garden can wait, cain't it?" William demanded.

His tone was one of which Nancy had never heard from him before, and she couldn't quite put her finger on what had got him so stirred up. He had been that way when he came home the night before.

Said he had been to the still, but Nancy didn't believe him. He was agitated then and he was still agitated this morning.

"I reckon it can," she said to William rather quietly as he slammed out the door.

Myra waited until she was sure he was gone before she crawled out of bed, got dressed and made her way to the kitchen where Nancy sat sipping on a cup of coffee. Nancy watched as Myra poured herself a cup and eased into the chair at the table. She looked to Nancy like she had been crying all night. Then Myra let out a small cry of pain when she picked up the hot cup. That's when Nancy noticed a large scrape on the palm of her hand.

"Alright missy, that's it. I wanna know what happened to you yesterdy," Nancy said sternly.

"I told you nothin'," Myra answered, looking down into the brown liquid in her cup.

"And I told you, I ain't standin' for that. Somethin' happened and if you don't tell me, I swear I'll find out from somebody else. You hear me, girl?" By this time Nancy had gotten to her feet, planted her hands on her hips and stared down at Myra.

Myra couldn't hold it in any longer. The tears began to flow again and she looked up at her mother and said, "I cain't tell you Ma. I just cain't."

"Yes, you can and you will, right here and now," Nancy said. "Did somebody hurt you Myra?"

Myra didn't answer, she just stared down into her cup.

"I said, did somebody hurt you?" Nancy was getting angry now at the thought that someone may have hurt her girl. She took Myra by the chin to face her. "Answer me!"

226

Myra knew she had to tell. "Yes Ma! Yes, somebody hurt me!"

Nancy sank back into her chair. The blood ran clean out of her face and she turned as pale as a ghost. "Who Myra? Who hurt you?"

"It was William, Ma! I swear it was William!"

Nancy had not heard Myra call him William since they had gotten married. From then on, he had been Pa to her and Cansada.

"What do you mean, it was William? What did he do to you?" she asked the question, but she really didn't want to hear the answer.

"He raped me, Ma. William raped me." With her words came the reality of it all and she sobbed uncontrollably.

Nancy went numb. Was it possible that this had really happened? That would certainly explain why William was acting the way he was when he got home last night and the way he was acting this morning.

"Are you sure, Myra?" Nancy knew that was a dumb question, but she had to ask it. Maybe Myra was just confused. Maybe it had been somebody else. But her mind told her otherwise. Maybe Myra was just making it all up. But why would she do such a thing?

Myra looked up at her mother and through her tears she whispered, "I'm sorry Ma. I really am. I didn't want to tell you. But it's true. He hurt me. He hurt me bad, Ma," she said, raising her dress so Nancy could see the scratches and bruises on her legs.

It was all too much for Nancy. She stared at Myra's legs, thinking about how her own husband could hurt the little girl he had fathered for all these years and wondering how she could have been so blind. She wanted to cry for her daughter, but no tears would come. Instead something welled up inside of her that she had never felt before, and it almost scared her. She was too calm. Her heart was pounding in her chest, as she got up from the table.

"Where you goin', Ma?" Myra asked through her sobs. She wiped the sleeve of her dress across her nose, watching her mother move slowly from the table to the fireplace.

Nancy took David's shotgun down from the mantel and checked to see if it was loaded.

"What are you gonna do, Ma?" Myra's eyes were wide with horror. "Ma, answer me. What are you gonna do?"

Myra was scared now. She had seen her mother mad before, but she had never seen her like this. She didn't look mad at all, she just looked calm and sad.

Nancy got to the door and turned to look at her daughter. The picture of yesterday's events clouded her mind and she said, "Don't you worry none. I'll be back soon."

She walked blindly for a short distance, unaware of her surroundings. Then she stopped and breathed in the fresh morning air. The birds were singing in the treetops and a small breeze whistled through the laurel. On any other day she would have found comfort in the woods around her. But on this day, nothing could fill the emptiness in her soul as she slowly made her way up the mountainside toward William's still.

Myra dried her eyes and walked out on the porch. She watched her mother till she was out of sight, then she sank down on the top step and waited. She knew that William would be furious at her for telling. But, what else was she supposed to do? She would never have blamed it on someone else, that just wouldn't be right, and already she had a feeling that she would probably bare a child for his evil.

Her thoughts ran in circles as she watched the place where she had last seen her mother. She knew William had a still on the mountain, but she wasn't sure where, and even if she knew where it was, she was too afraid to go there now.

The sun rose in the heavens. Myra prepared dinner but didn't eat with Commodore and Cansada. Instead she wondered in and out of the house looking toward the mountain.

Finally she caught a glimpse of Nancy coming out of the woods. Myra watched as she made her way along the edge of the field to the trail that led to the cemetery. Since moving here, they had spent many hours in the little cemetery, keeping the weeds chopped down and putting flowers on the stones. It was a special place for all of them, but Myra knew it was particularly special to Nancy.

It was suppertime before Nancy got back to the house. Myra met her at the door. "Are you alright, Ma? What happened?"

Nancy placed the shotgun back above the fireplace. She always knew there was more than one reason David had taught her how to use that thing. She turned and took Myra by both shoulders, looked her straight in the eyes, and smiled. "Now, don't you worry none, you hear. Ain't nobody gonna ever hurt you again."

She hugged her close.

"But, what about William? Is he mad Ma? I know he's mad at me? I'm so sorry."

Nancy let Myra go and faced her again. "He ain't mad and he won't be comin' back here. You'll never ever have to look at him again. And don't you ever be sorry, 'cause there ain't nothin' for you to be sorry for."

Myra started to protest.

"I said, there ain't nothin' to be sorry for," Nancy said again, sternly. "Now, go and git me some supper 'for I starve to death."

She sank down in a chair at the table and waited for Myra to bring her a plate of food. The days events had taken a lot out of her, but she was damn sure that William wouldn't be bothering Myra again and for that she was thankful.

Everybody on Ellijay wondered where William had taken off to and, after several weeks, began asking Nancy and the kids about him. But nobody seemed to know. Last time Nancy had seen him, she told Abe and Lydia, he was going to the still. He was supposed to have come home and helped her plant the garden but never showed up. She went to the still looking for him, but he wasn't there. She hadn't said nothing about it because he had been mad about something when he left the house, and she just figured he was cooling off somewhere and would eventually come home.

Nancy didn't know if anyone believed her or not and she could care less one way or the other. Most folks just figured he ran off with another woman, seeing as how he was so much younger than Nancy. "That poor little Nancy," the women of Ellijay talked. "Seems like bad luck just follows her everyplace she goes."

Nancy heard their whispers and figured it was best to let them think what they wanted to think. Right now her concerns were about Myra. How was she going to explain this baby to the neighbors? Nobody could ever know that it belonged to William, least not while she was living.

She knew she would have to take Myra away, and the only place she knew to go was to Tiger, Georgia, where Frank and Martha Parker lived. Frank and Martha were distant kinfolks of David's. He had always thought highly of them. They had visited them on several occasions before David went into the war and, after he died, Martha had written Nancy often, asking her to bring the children and come live in Georgia.

"I'm takin' the younguns to see Frank and Martha for a spell," she told Bill one day.

Bill knew his mother had been distant since William had left. For the life of him, he couldn't figure out why William would just take off like that. He and Bill had been friends for years, and Bill thought that, surely, he would have known if William had another woman. Myra had seemed particularly unhappy about William's leaving, at least that's what Bill thought. But Myra was sad because she knew she was carrying her stepfather's baby, and she was afraid everybody would find out.

That June was one of the hottest Nancy could remember as she and Commodore, Cansada, Retta and Myra pulled the old wagon onto the road and headed off Ellijay. If everything went well, they would be in Tiger the next day. She had written Martha to tell her they were coming. She just hoped there wouldn't be no questions about William.

But, of course, there was. That was the first thing Martha asked her. "Now where's that young man a yours, you been a tellin' me about all these years?"

Before Nancy could answer, Myra spoke up, "He ain't comin'. He's got too much work to do in the fields and all."

"But Pa ain't home," seven-year-old Commodore said, jumping from the back of the wagon. "He ain't been home in a long time."

"Hush up Commodore," Nancy scolded.

Martha looked at her in question.

"Awe, it ain't nothin'," Nancy said. "He's just run off for a spell. He'll be back."

"Now, ain't that somethin' else," Martha said, shaking her head. "Man gets him a fine woman, then leaves her to tend the children while he gallivants around. I just don't know about 'em, do you?"

"Nope," Nancy said. "Ain't never been able to figure no man out before and probably never will. Gonna quit tryin', that's what I'm gonna do. Just gonna quit tryin'."

Both women laughed as they went in the house.

Nancy stayed in Georgia until fall colors began to form on the horizon. She knew she had to get back to Ellijay before winter set in, and Myra would be having the baby in just a few short months. Retta had been courting one of Tiger's local boys and she didn't want to leave. She was 22 years old, so Nancy couldn't rightly make her do anything she didn't want to, so she agreed to let her stay, at least for the winter.

By the time Bill had finished making the cane syrup, Nancy was back home. She left Retta to live in a small shack on Martha and Frank's property and hoped that she would fair well through the winter and come back to Ellijay in the spring.

"What in tar nation?" Abe called out when he saw Nancy trying to help Myra out of the wagon.

"Give me a hand, will you, Abe?" Nancy asked. "Myra done went and got herself a biscuit in the oven since we been gone."

"I see that," Abe said, helping Myra down from the wagon. "And, just where might the young feller be?"

"There ain't no young feller," Myra answered, looking down at her dust covered shoes.

"Now hold on here just a minute," Abe said, squinting his eyes.

"Not now, Abe," Nancy said, knowing that Abe would be having lot's of questions if she let him keep talking, and she wasn't in the mood to answer anything.

Commodore bounced down from the wagon, " Is Pa home?"

Nancy hadn't thought about it before, but she was sure that Commodore figured his Pa would be home by now. She knew the boy missed his Pa, but there wasn't anything she could do about it. Eventually he would realize that William wasn't coming home and he could hate him for it if he wanted to as far as she was concerned.

Abe lifted the boy up on his shoulders and spun him around. "Nope, your Pa ain't home," he said.

"Why not?" Commodore giggled as Abe continued to spin him.

"Don't rightly know," he answered, looking at Nancy.

"Well, don't look at me Mr. Abe Moore. How am I sposed to know why he ain't here? And, furthermore, I don't care that he ain't here. Probably done found him a little hussy somewhere and that suits me just fine, it does."

Nancy lifted her skirts and stomped off into the house with Myra trailing behind her. She didn't have to answer nobody's questions and they may as well leave her well enough alone. She felt herself stiffen at the thought of people buttin' into her business.

But it was just a matter of time before Lydia did just that. First, she wanted to know who the father of Myra's baby was. Then, in the same breath, she wanted to know if Nancy knew what had happened to William. The answer to the first question was that she didn't know and Myra wasn't telling anybody. The answer to the second question was that she didn't know and she didn't care.

Lydia had known Nancy all her life and she knew her mother. So she wasn't taking any of this lightly. She kept prodding at Nancy like an old sow, until Nancy flew mad at her.

"Lydia, it ain't none a your business!" she yelled at her one day. Her feet were planted firmly and, for a split second, Nancy thought about pushing the old woman off the porch.

"Now, Nancy, don't you go gettin' all fired up at me. People's a talkin', they is. All over Ellijay. They sayin' bad thangs 'bout you and Myra, and I don't like it."

"Well, I don't like it either," Nancy said. "But there just ain't nothin' I can do about it, now is there? Best thang for you to do, is stay out of it."

She spit her wad of snuff off the porch and walked back in the house.

"Well, I ain't never," Lydia said under her breath as she stomped down the steps. There was something going on, she just knew it. But she also knew she would never hear what it was from Nancy. That woman was more set in her ways than anybody Lydia had ever known and she knew that she may as well just let it go.

On a freezing January day in 1880, Rosetta Parker was born. Myra screamed in pain as her daughter came into the world. But, once she held her in her arms, the pain of her birth disappeared, as did the pain of her conception. She would love this child despite what everyone said and, someday, she would find a descent man that would take care of them both.

All over Ellijay, folks had their own theory about what had happened to William. Some even put two and two together and thought they not only knew what happened to William, but they knew why, once Rosetta was born. All they had to do was count the months to figure it out. But wasn't none of them saying any such thing to Nancy. No, siree. That was one woman to be feared, and they were more sure of that now than they had ever been.

Long about spring, Nancy decided it was time for her to go back to Georgia and see how Retta was doing. She made the trip with Commodore and Cansada, leaving Myra behind to tend to the baby.

She just wasn't sure when she would be coming back. She was in no hurry. She figured the longer she stayed away, the quieter all the talk would get.

She moved into the little house with Retta and stayed until Retta married Bill Barrett, the boy she had been courting. Then she decided it was time to go back home. Cansada was already 15 and Nancy knew that, before long, she too would find a man and leave her household. She just hoped he would be from Ellijay so she would always be close to her. One by one her children were growing up, and Nancy felt lonely again.

Talk had settled down some when Nancy returned to Ellijay and Myra had stepped right into motherhood. She had shut a lot of folks up by telling them that the baby's pa lived in Georgia and had promised to come get her when he found out about Rosetta. This kept folks happy for a spell, but it still didn't keep them from wondering about William. They would always wonder, but they would never really know.

In 1883, Nancy finally sent Commodore to school at Mountain Grove. She had hoped to send him earlier, but found that she needed him at home when William was no longer around. Already he was 10 years old, and she had to send him now if he were to ever learn how to read and write.

He was a smart little feller and stayed in school a couple of years. But as he got older, it seemed he had rambling in his blood. He just couldn't stay still, and there wasn't much for him to do on Ellijay. Occasionally, he would walk through the woods to his father's old still. He wished he would have been old enough to learn how to make moonshine when his Pa was still around. He would run his hand over the old twisted coil of the still and wonder what happened to his pa. Nancy never talked about him, and after awhile, neither did any of the other younguns. One thing was certain, he could feel his pa's blood running through him and he felt an urge to move off the mountain.

Finally, when he was 16, he did just that. Commodore left Ellijay and went to Retta's. Then, from there, he went on into Burton, Georgia, where he met a bunch of bootleggers who were more than willing to teach him the moonshining trade. Nancy wasn't none too happy about his decision, but there was nothing she could do about it, except pray that the revenuers didn't catch him.

Myra stayed with Nancy until Rosetta was about 10 years old. Then she married a man who loved her enough to claim Rosetta as his own. They built a cabin on Mountain Grove, at the head of Ellijay. Cansada still lived with Nancy, who was now 60 years old, and still a spitfire like she had always been. She may not move as fast, but she could still put out a garden and do the cooking and cleaning. At least she wasn't alone. She was surrounded by most of her children, though Margaret Alice was still in Burnsville, and Retta and Commodore were in Georgia.

Just out of the blue one day, Nancy decided she wanted to go back to Georgia for awhile. The kids didn't much need her anymore, and she had a hankering to see Retta and Commodore. Bill and Charlie pleaded with her not to go. They thought she was too old to travel that far.

"I ain't that old," she told them both as they hitched up her wagon. "I can take care of myself. Always have, always will. Besides, Cansada will be with me."

She was as stubborn as an old mule, and the boys knew that nothing they said would make her stay if she had her mind set on leaving. So they let her go. She stayed for a while with Retta, then went on to Burton to see Commodore. He was frazzled, to say the least, and she knew he was so caught up in the business that she may never get him back. He smoked big cigars, wore fancy clothes and talked like a grown man. She was concerned and she wrote Bill and told him those concerns.

Bill was a fine Christian man and he didn't want no brother of his getting into any trouble, so he set down and wrote Commodore a letter:

Ellijay N.C. 7-17-91
J.C. Robinson
Burton, Ga.
Dear Brother,
   ... We have the best crop we ever had. Our oats are good. You ought to come back here and work in the mines. Dr. Lucus is working about 15 hands at Brond Minceys mine. He has worked all summer there. This season has been the closest time for money I ever saw.
   We are having a fine Sunday School at Mountain Grove. Come out and go with me to the association third Sunday in august ...

Come when you can come.

From your big brother

J.W.P

Commodore read the letter out loud.

"I ain't workin' in no mines," he said, snarling his nose at the very idea of such.

"But thank about it," Nancy told him. "If you stay here, them revenuers will surely catch up with you. You can go back to Ellijay and work in the mines and still make moonshine. I'll even show you where your pa's old still is. Maybe you can fix it up."

He knew where his pa's still was, and he knew his mother was right. So, Commodore went back to Ellijay. Nancy and Cansada stayed in Georgia. Nancy just wasn't quite ready to leave yet. Around these parts nobody knew her and everybody left her alone. That's what she liked. That's what she had always wanted, for people to just not bother her.

Each time Nancy left Ellijay, she would pack all her belongings in the old trunk and take it with her. It was the same trunk she had taken from Granny Stuart's, when she and David moved to Cane Branch. It was the same trunk she had taken from there to Ellijay when she was ran off her property. All of her personal possessions fit into this one trunk, and the possessions that meant the most to her, she decided, should always be with her. On many occasions she would take David's letters from the trunk and read them, wondering where she would be if he were still alive. Sometimes she would take out the long strands of her mother's hair and find comfort in its touch. Every now and again she would even read the poem the hair was wrapped in and wonder what her mother was thinking when she wrote it. These things were all she had left from the people she had loved most in her life.

Commodore moved in with Bill and began working in the mines. But he also got William's still back to running. He had been gone from Georgia for little more than a year when the revenuers came through and arrested several of his moonshining buddies, including some from Ellijay. It was common practice for them to make the moonshine in the mountains and have runners carry it south to sale in the larger cities. Commodore was no longer running the shine, but he was definitely making it. Nancy figured that some of the liquor that had been confiscated could have been his.

She felt a need, stronger than she had ever felt before, to get her youngest boy out of the business once and for all. She thought that, just maybe, if she wrote him a letter telling him about his friends, he would listen to her. She opened the trunk and took her mother's hair from the paper. Maybe if he read the words his own grandmother had written from her jail cell -- *But oh that dreadful judge I fear, Shall I that awful sentence hear, Depart ye cursed down to hell, And forever there to dwell* -- he would consider giving up the moonshining business before he ended up in jail too.

She touched the hair to her cheek, then wrapped it in a handkerchief and put it back in the trunk.

Then she took her pen and began to write on the faded paper:

Oct 2 1892

Mr. J.C. Robinson

> *Dear Sir I take the opportunity of writeing to you inform you that I am well at the present time hope you are enjoying*

the same blessing. I have got my fodder safe. Well Comadore the revenuw has got A.N.W and Robert Watts, Lenard Cathey and Frank Cathey. But they turned Frank loose at Gainesville. Sent the other boyes to Atlanta jail. Kinney bragg has bin off with a load of apples. He got 75 cents and $100 per bushel. I now under stand the revenew has got Mack McClain. They got Thomas Bramlett, but he got away. They got Thomas at Bob Dennys in the field at Work.

William (Bill) write how Will Grigry has got and how Vasti has got. Sarah Benfield has got her a fine girl 5 day of September hit was borned. Susie Teemes has hir a fine boy. William hurry and get your house done come and fix my house for me. The people is all about dun foddering and sowing grane.

Comadore, Seny King has run away with her a man. The have bin gown about 10 dayes. They say they went to North Calina. We do not know where they went to. So I will close.

Your mother Nancy Robison
Write and give us all the news

Commodore read the letter, then he read the poem he had heard often from his mother. He knew exactly why she had written to him, and he knew why it was on the paper with the poem. It didn't make him give up making moonshine though, but he did quit running it back and fourth to Georgia.

Bill finished building his new house the following spring and went to Georgia to see what kind of fixing up Nancy's house needed. Retta and her husband had built them a new house, and Nancy and Cansada were still living in the little shack. But he didn't know it was in as bad a shape as it was.

"Ma, you need to come home," Bill told her as he watched drops of water fall from the ceiling into an iron pot Nancy had set on the floor.

"This is home," she said.

"No, it's not Ma and it never was," he answered, rubbing his forehead. "And it's about to fall in."

"Well, it's the only home I got right now," she argued.

He reached over and took her wrinkled hands in his. "My, how she has aged," he thought, touching them to his face.

She jerked her hands away from him and plunged them into her apron pockets, "Now don't go to goin' soft on me, boy," she scolded.

He knew how she was, so he just smiled and said, "I ain't a goin' soft on you, Ma. I just want you to come back to Ellijay where we can look after you."

"Don't need no lookin' after," she said firmly.

"Ok." Bill urged. "Then come back because we all need you to look after us and help us with them grandyounguns of yourn."

"That's more like it," she smiled when she thought of the little ones running around. She missed little hands tugging at her dress hem. "I been a thinkin' maybe I ought to. I ain't got nobody here 'cept Retta, and she could come see me as easy in North Calina as she can here. Let me thank on it for a spell."

"Well, if you decide to come back with me, you and Cansada can live in my old house in Mountain Grove. It'd make you a fine home, Ma. It shore would indeed."

That night, Nancy lay in bed, wide awake, thinking about going back to Ellijay. Seemed like she would always end up back on that mountain. But it wasn't so bad. That's where most all her family was and she liked it there. If it hadn't been for William, she would have never left there to begin with. By now most of the folks that had told all them tales was dead and gone anyway, and those that were left had probably forgotten about it by now. She needed to be with her grandchildren, and she needed to be back on her mountain.

Nancy drifted off to sleep, knowing that she would soon be back home, and this time, she would never leave.

CHAPTER FOURTEEN
1894–1901

It wasn't long after Nancy and Cansada moved back to Ellijay that Cansada met Jesse G. Owens. She was 29 years old and had always lived with her mother. Actually, she was a lot like her mother. She was a little backward when it came to people, and she preferred to be left alone. After she and Owens wed, they stayed on Ellijay, close to Nancy.

Commodore went back to Georgia and married a girl he had met there before. He continued making moonshine, but visited Nancy often.

Bill's old house set on a little hill surrounded by woods, just above the Mountain Grove Road that led across Onion Mountain. There were several neighbors, Nancy just couldn't see them from the house. The little, white boarded Mountain Grove Church and schoolhouse were just down the road a piece. Nancy stood on the porch and took it all in. This was the nicest house she had ever lived in. There were no leaks in the roof, and no cracks in the walls for snow to blow through. "Surely, this must be my heaven," she thought, breathing in the fresh mountain air, "or the good Lord wouldn't keep bringin' me back here."

She closed her eyes and remembered how she had felt that day so long ago, when she and David had walked up the side of the mountain in Cane Branch. "Right here's where we'll build our house," he said to her. Those were the happiest days of her life and she could almost feel his arms around her waist.

"Oh, that's just silly thinkin'," she scolded herself out loud. But, already, her eyes were clouded with tears. It wasn't silly at all. Those good memories were all she had to hold onto. If she let them go, she would have nothing.

Day in and day out, Nancy sat on her porch and rocked, thinking about her life. It had been a hard life at times, but somehow she had gotten through it all and raised her children. Now she was alone, but she wasn't lonely. Every day on her way to school, Myra's second daughter, Peggy, would carry a bucket of water in for her. Every day Bill or Charlie would come by to see her.

"You got any of them biscuits left?" Bill would ask, rubbing his belly. "I'm mighty hungry."

Nancy would fuss as she wrapped leftover biscuits in a cloth for him to carry home. "Ain't that wife a yourn learned to make biscuits yet?" she would tease.

Bill would smile and pat his mother on the shoulder as she told him to "get on outta here now and leave me alone."

One day, however, she said to him, "Bill, you know, I been a thinkin',"

"What is it now, old woman?" He teased.

But Nancy was serious. "The best years of my life was with your pa, you know?"

"I know, Ma. You've always said that," Bill said, wondering what Nancy was thinking.

"Well, when I leave this here mountain, it'd only be fittin' to have his name on my grave stone."

"Now, don't go talkin' like that, Ma. You ain't goin' nowhere any time soon."

"But, you know what I'm a sayin' son. I'll always be Nancy Parker, and when I'm dead and gone, that's how I want folks to remember me."

"If you say so, Ma." He patted her on the shoulder. "Whatever you want."

She knew he would make sure she got what she wanted, he always did. He was so much like his pa, always looking out for her and making sure she was happy.

And she was -- at least for awhile.

Shortly after Cansada married, she was with child. Nancy looked forward to the day she could help birth a grandbaby. She sure wished Aunt Sinda was here. They had kept in touch through the years, but both were too old to travel now. Nancy could just hear Sinda saying, "Now you just get outta the way and let Aunt Sinda bring this here baby in the world."

But it wasn't meant to be. The baby tried to come early, and before Nancy could even get to Cansada, she had lost them both. It was an overwhelming sadness for Nancy. She had lost a lot of people in her life, but never a child, and this was the child that David never even knew he had. She thought her old heart would surely stop beating. But she went on, just like she always had.

Nancy's life was quite a mystery, and maybe that's why folks mostly considered her strange and left her to herself. But there were things about her life that even she would never truly know or understand. One thing was certain though, her mother did kill her father and was hanged for it. She had heard so many tales through the years that she would never know what really happened that night as she lay sleeping in her cradle. No one would ever know.

She would never understand why the Silvers took her property when it was the only thing she ever owned in her life. And she would surely never understand why William done what he did. She knew she should of never married him. One thing was certain, though; she knew what happened to William, but no one else ever would. She just figured it best to put all that behind her and live out her final days in the sweet serenity this mountain offered.

In 1899 her boy, Charlie, left his family heading to Georgia to see Commodore. He never got there and was never heard from again. Nancy never knew if he was dead or alive, but once again, gossip spread throughout the mountains. Nancy hoped that would be the last heartbreak she had to endure.

She had kept good health through most of her life, but it began fading soon after Charlie left. Her wrinkled hands showed that of hard labor in the fields and the creases in her face showed a woman desperate to find true peace.

Fall was approaching the mountains surrounding Macon County. The leaves had not yet began to color, but Nancy could feel it in the air as a cool breeze came through the lifted window of her bedroom. She had never smelled the wind before, but on this day, it seemed to bring an essence of honeysuckle into the room.

She closed her eyes to savor the moment, taking one last deep breath of the fresh morning air. Then she found the peace she had searched for all her life, September 20, 1901, at home on Mountain Grove.

Her children buried her in the cemetery next to the little white church, and as all the community folk watched, Myra laid the locket of long, dark hair on Nancy's casket.

Top left is Nancy's grave at Mountain Grove Baptist Church in
Franklin, NC. Her tombstone reads: Nancy Parker Nov. 3, 1830 –
Sept. 20, 1901 Gone but not forgotten. The memorial at the foot of
her grave is for her husband David Parker (pictured right). It
reads: In memory of Nancy's husband PVT David W. Parker CSA
NC 54th Co B Born 1827 – Died April 14, 1865 Buried Hollywood
Cemetery Richmond, Virginia.

CONCLUSION

This book contains stories handed down from the Stuart side of Frankie Silver's family. Some of the names used are indeed the real names of certain characters, some are fiction.

Barbara Stuart's legal custody papers for Nancy read exactly as quoted in this book.

The lease, which Nancy made with Edward Boone, contains her real signature and can be seen at the Burnsville, NC courthouse; proving that she could write.

All of the letters that David Parker wrote Nancy during his time in the Civil War are in the Parker family. Several of these letters appear in italics, exactly as written, in this book, as does the letter that she wrote to her son, Commodore. The original letter to Commodore is written on the stationary containing the poem that Frankie Silver supposedly read at her hanging. It is unproven whether she wrote the poem or not, and no one knows for certain that she read the poem aloud.

The actual court records and deeds have been discovered, also at the Burnsville courthouse, to prove Nancy's land was taken from her for the $1.20 that she owed the dentist.

Aunt Sinda was the daughter of Will Griffen and worked at the Nu Wray Inn in Burnsville. The inn was built in 1833 and is still in operation today as a bed and breakfast.

Fifty women did indeed raid the warehouse of Government supplies in Burnsville in 1864, before Kirk's Raiders got there. We believe that Nancy could have been among those 50 women, but have no documentation of proof.

Nancy left her daughter, Margaret Alice, behind in Burnsville. The story handed down in the Stuart family is that Margaret Alice was staying with a friend and Nancy didn't have time to get her before the wagon train left. Margaret Alice lived in that area until her death in 1957.

There has always been a mystery surrounding the disappearance of William C. Robinson, Nancy's second husband. It has never been a secret that he raped his stepdaughter Myra. Some family stories claim that he was never seen again after the rape because he left Macon County, while others claim that Nancy killed him. Mountain Grove's 1883 school attendance records show that Commodore was attending school there, and his mother was listed as "widow, Nancy Robinson." This would have been three years after William disappeared. To our knowledge, no death record has been found for him.

Nancy's son, Charlie, left Macon County to see his brother in Georgia in 1899 and wasn't heard from again until about 100 years later, when his great-grandson by the same name, Charlie Parker, was discovered living in Texas. According to him, his great-grandfather moved there from Macon County and started a new family. It is unsure what his reasons for leaving were.

The hair that Nancy kept with her belonged to her mother, Frankie. Through the years, several family members talked about seeing the long, black hair that Myra kept in a quart jar after Nancy died. According to Myra's daughter, Minnie, after Myra died in 1949, she and her sister, Sally, found the jar of hair and buried it next to Myra's home place in Mountain Grove.

Nancy's headstone reads: Nancy Parker.

There are no known photographs of Nancy Silver Parker.

CPSIA information can be obtained at www.ICGtesting.com
Printed in the USA
BVOW011840310113

312105BV00010B/267/P